DANCER DAWKINS
AND THE CALIFORNIA KID

CLASSICS OF ASIAN AMERICAN LITERATURE

WILLYCE KIM FOREWORD BY EUNSONG KIM

Dancer Dawkins and the California Kid

WITH A NEW PREFACE

University of Washington Press / Seattle

Dancer Dawkins and the California Kid was made possible in part by a grant from the Shawn Wong Book Fund, which supports the publication of books on Asian American history and culture.

UNIVERSITY OF WASHINGTON PRESS uwapress.uw.edu

♾ This paper meets the requirements of ANSI/NISO z39.48-1992 (Permanence of Paper).

THIS BOOK IS DEDICATED TO

THE MEMORY OF EMMA PEEL

AND TO PHOENIX

I WOULD LIKE TO THANK

KITTY TSUI, CAROL PERKINS,

BARBARA S. BULL,

MY THERAPIST,

AND THE MAKERS OF B-COMPLEX

Foreword

LOOKING FOR THE DYKES WHO LONGED
FOR AN AMERIKAN REVOLUTION

I always want to know how women love. I want to know how they loved each other, how they expressed their loves, and how they learned to fight those that kept them from their loves. How did queer women of color organize, grieve, revolt, and love before me? How did they do this last year, and the year before that, and in the time prior? It feels vital to know about the political lineage one wishes to be part of—how does one pursue this without the reactionary politics imbued inside *nostalgia*?

The past is too often invoked as a referent for nostalgia, a marker for a mythic time that never was and can no longer be.[1] Nostalgics have a selected era, a preferred and ideal time they wish to return to—a collapsed cloistering of some curated past for their future gain. White supremacists point to the affordability of homes in the forties with no mention of segregation; misogynists to a homeland where only men rule. One can reject this venal politics of nostalgia and still take up a recuperative project that queries toward some past in the form of representation, a past that remains unknown and imbued with longing.

Cautiously tending to this desire, I spent the summer of 2022 reading the archives of writers I admired. I wanted to know whom they corresponded with, how they paid their bills, and whom and how they fought. With careful consideration and the desire to learn about the development of their poetics, I wanted to know: whom did they consider their community, and how did they love each other?

In the midst of this search I found letters from Willyce Kim to Pat Parker. In an undated letter Willyce Kim writes to her friend, "what the hell is wrong with us romantic poets? . . . I am out of my mind, wildly in love with the woman. I don't even know what the word self-protection means." Included in the letter is a portrait of Willyce from her book *eating artichokes* and two poems, "The next woman" and one from *Under the Rolling Sky*. The letter concludes with lines from "The next woman," which read:

And when we love,
I promise you love
How we will love to love
Each other's loves . . .

followed by the statement "Here's what I wish for the both of you."[2]

The line "How we will love to love / Each other's loves" speaks to a commitment to consider not just the present but the past and future of one's beloved. It is anti-nostalgic; it is present full. The speaker in the poem marks against the isolation required to idealize one's beloved as just one's own and instead looks toward the unknown process of surrendering to all facets of the other's desires. The woman in love and the woman being loved believes the adventure has already begun and enters her spaces without the impulse of new creation, and through the complexities required of everything else.

———

Divided into prose poem–esque blocks, Willyce Kim's *Dancer* *Dawkins and the California Kid* introduces us to the worlds of Dancer Dawkins, the California Kid (Wilhelmina Jennings "Little Willy" Gutherie), Jessica Nahale Riggins, Bucky Benton, Roxie Austin, and Ta Jan (Penelope Frances Lee). At the onset, we are introduced to glimpses of their childhood, the various part-time jobs the women have held or currently hold, and what their relationships are like. We learn that these characters are without a hint of deference to cultural norms or decorum, and through this rebellion, their intimacies as friends and lovers become fortified. Because we learn so much about their complexities and contradictions as characters, we are prepared to follow them on a series of acts that involve infiltration, deception, poisoning, sex, a deux ex machina in the form of a German shepherd, and retribution against the evil forces of the ruling corporate overlords.

The backdrop of this adventure takes place at the infamous Bohemian Grove. In the section titled "Fortune" we witness Ta Jan asking the others what they know about "The Bohemians," who, as "some of the wealthiest men in the nation," come together every summer to make secret deals in the redwoods of California. Once embroiled in a discrimination lawsuit for its "only male members allowed" policy, the Grove, which has included the likes of presidents Reagan, Nixon, and both Bushes, is rumored to have been where Oppenheimer and others planned the rapacious, world-altering Manhattan Project. Founded in 1878 and fitting neatly into contemporary conspiracies of the deep state, the Bohemian Grove sits to this day at 20601 Bohemian Avenue, where it remains a floating presence of all that has yet to change: backroom deals for the already powerful and a consolidation of corporate and state power, with a firm lock on the distinction between those on the inside and those willfully excluded. What is often underdescribed by these tales is the white male supremacist formations of this class and how the harms they enact have a clear direction: they target and prey upon the most vulnerable, devastating the lives and communities of those already dispossessed from land and property, those once understood as colonized—such as Ta Jan's family lineage. The sole Korean character of the novel, Ta Jan describes her family's immigration history within the lineage of 1910–1925 Korean "picture brides" sent to Hawaii, linking how the history of Japanese colonization and US imperialism have shaped the disparate communities of exiles and migrants, whose lives are foundational to the malediction also called America. While few are exempt from the harms of US oligarchs, their violence is directed first and foremost toward poor nonwhite communities and queer persons outside the bounds of *moral subjectivity*; thus, to imagine the takedown of "The Bohemians" by loosely employed lesbians: a fucking triumph.

In theorizing women of color feminism and the critique

queer women's writing enacts, Grace Hong describes how the works of Cherríe Moraga agitate how nation-state morality becomes naturalized in even the particularized spaces of Chicano and queer formations. Writing on what normative morality offers, Hong states, "Being a moral subject means having claims to protection from necropolitical violence, to having a claim to exist, and for one's existence to be protected." It is through one's conscription into moral subjectivity that the state offers "protection," and the refusal to subscribe to it is met with legislated precarity. Cautioning how in our neoliberal era, moral conscription expands diversely across race, gender, and sexuality, Hong suggests that "it is precisely in the condition of being unprotected that we find alternative expressions of the political. . . . These alternative expressions are . . . unrecognizable as politics, because the notion of the political has been so thoroughly captured by the pursuit of protection of life."[3]

As tangentially employed lesbians with no dreams for normative ascendancies, Ta Jan, Dancer Dawkins, and the Kid configure explorations of queer formations unbound by the checks and balances of propriety. And thus, if examined uncarefully, their politics might be obscured. Dancer and the Kid enter a compound to rescue Jessica. There, they are met with violence and temporarily lose the fight, with Dancer and Jessica becoming hostages. In the efforts toward their escape and in order to enact retribution against the organization's boss, Ta Jan—considered by the racists to be unassuming and unthreatening—sets up a plan to infiltrate the compound by feigning to poison Fatin Satin Aspen. While escaping, the group encounters a map of areas to be sprayed with a toxin and repositions the designation labels so that the Bohemian Grove will instead be its target.

Willyce tells me that the backdrop of the poisoning and the toxic spraying is informed by the presence of Agent Orange in news and media during the 1960s and '70s. Richard Nixon, president during the Vietnam War, was a member of the Bohemian Grove and is thought to have prolonged war efforts; and in 1962, John F. Kennedy, also a member of the group, dumped Agent Orange into forests in Vietnam, Cambodia, and Laos.[4] Due to their efforts, it is estimated that at least 4 million people in Vietnam were exposed to the poison, not to mention its other environmental and potential unknown effects. Thus, when the lesbian infiltrators weaponize the historical backdrop and narrative potency of Agent Orange against its rumored originators, what we get is the political pleasure of the revenge of representation.

Every part of this novel—the adventure, its refusal of heteronormative refinement, and its politicized revenge fantasies—falls outside of familiar expectations for Asian American and lesbian narratives. Here, identity, sexuality, life, and politics are not fixed, fetishistic markers of decoration but one part of the ongoing formation toward *queer futurity*.[5] The novel and its speakers remove themselves from a straight plane that demands they articulate their positions to it. The characters are without linear coming-out confessions, nor do they partake in ethnic informancy. The language of the novel invites neither white nor normative sympathies. Yet the language too refuses the temptations of a postracial aesthetic in the form of denial: the characters are lesbians, some characters are racialized as Korean and *hapa* from Hawai'i, and the characters are full of familial longing and political ambitions for their worlds to thrive—nothing is denied, contrived, forced, or pleading for the gaze of acceptance.

In discussing the function of realism and the tradition of the "great novel" on Asian American writers, Lisa Lowe writes, "the imposition of the colonial language and its cultural institutions, among them the novel, demands the subject's internalization of 'superiority' of the colonizer and the 'inferiority' of the colonized, even as it attempts to evacuate the subject of 'native' language, traditions, and practices."[6] Rather than surrendering to such expectations, Lowe argues that this interaction produces "contradictory subjects" where the Asian American writer develops through an antagonistic relationship to the colonial language. And in describing the possibilities of queer form, John Keene suggests that such form "pushes against and destabilizes usual norms and conventions."[7] *Dancer Dawkins and the California Kid* stretches the limits of how queer forms and Asian American antagonisms have previously been examined. No politics is declarative, no identity stable. The work asks us to imagine how the Asian American writer may push us both toward and against preexisting formations. In a roundtable on Asian American studies in the twenty-first century," Lowe wondered

how to mobilize the study of Asian Americans in a way that it doesn't aspire to assimilate to whiteness . . . doesn't aspire to be a unit in the social reproduction of the same. But is guided by these principles of transformation, and interrogating how we know what we know . . . there's a lot of potential but maybe it won't be called Asian

American studies. Maybe it will be called the history of everything.[8]

Likewise, perhaps *Dancer Dawkins and the California Kid* will challenge us toward this history, whereby in exhausting the limits of preexisting identity categories, it asks for the *history of everything* to be felt, explored, and cared for.

———

Willyce Kim, who grew up in Hawaii, moved to San Francisco for college and never left. During and after college she lived and congregated with lesbian writers in Oakland, touring the West Coast with the likes of Pat Parker, Audre Lorde, and Judy Grahn for poetry readings, and partaking in events such as "Dykes for an Amerikan Revolution," hosted by Janice Mirikitani and the Glide Church with Nancy Adair, Brenda Crider, and others. When asked where they read and how they traveled, Willyce tells me, "We would procure a working car, and travel up and down the California coast, into Oregon and Washington, reading our poems." In 1974 Willyce was featured prominently on the cover of *Lesbians Speak Out*. Her activism and poetry span generations and pull together intimate networks that continue to remain outside of mainstream discourse.

When I ask Willyce about her involvement with various poetry circles and her thoughts on the history and status of queer and Asian American writing and activism, she provides me with no definitive statements. From her longtime work with the Women's Press Collective, her knowledge and experience with lesbian housing spaces throughout the Bay, and her involvement in queer multiethnic communities of support and kinship,[9] if anyone were to have judgments or hold declarative critiques about the past and future, I would accept them from Willyce. Instead, during my brief time interviewing her about the book and her life, she embodied an antinostalgic stance and approached my questions about her past without sentimentality. Rather than lecturing me about the past and about her work, she sat across from me open, porous, and ready to learn. She asked me so many questions that I wondered if we would ever know about all that she's done, all that she's been involved with, and if this opacity toward self is part of what allows for her work to remain activated.

The language of *Dancer Dawkins* and the porousness of Willyce's presence illuminate all that remains possible in the life of the novel for its many readers to come.

Eunsong Kim

NOTES

1. Saidiya Hartman writes critically against the romanticizing of archives that hold official records on chattel slavery to reconstruct the past. Her writing is instructive to all archival pursuit and a critical wondering into pasts obscured, for better and worse. See "Venus in Two Acts," *Small Axe* 12, no. 2 (June 2008): 1–14.

2. Pat Parker Archives, Box 4, Schlesinger Library, Harvard University.

3. Grace Hong, "Existentially Surplus: Women of Color Feminism and the New Crises of Capitalism," *GLQ: A Journal of Lesbian and Gay Studies* 18, no. 1 (January 2012): 87–106. Hong writes about moral subjects again in *Death beyond Disavowal: The Impossible Politics of Difference* (Minneapolis: University of Minnesota Press, 2015), 65.

4. Colin Schultz, "Nixon Prolonged Vietnam War for Political Gain—And Johnson Knew About It, Newly Unclassified Tapes Suggest," *Smithsonian Magazine*, March 18, 2013, accessed online; Andrew Glass, "This Day in Politics: U.S. Launches Spraying of Agent Orange, Jan. 18, 1962," *Politico*, January 18, 2019, https://www.politico.com/story/2019/01/18/us-launches-operation-ranch -hand-jan-18-1962-1102346.

5. I'm pulling this notion from José Esteban Muñoz, who operationalized the term in *Cruising Utopia: The Then and There of Queer Futurity* (New York: NYU Press, 2009).

6. Lisa Lowe, *Immigrant Acts: On Asian American Cultural Politics* (Durham, NC: Duke University Press, 1996), 97.

7. Reginald Harris, "John Keene: On Hidden Histories and Why Writing against Official Narratives Is Queer," *Lambda Literary*, June 3, 2015, http://www .lambdaliterary.org/interviews/06/03/john-keene-on-hidden-histories-and -why-writing-against-official-narratives-is-queer/.

8. Yale Center for the Study of Race, Indigeneity, and Transnational Migration, "Asian American Studies in the 21st Century," panel discussion with Lisa Lowe, Cathy J. Schlund-Vials, and Gary Okihiro, moderated by Daniel HoSang, introduction by Quan Tran.

9. Pat Parker describes Willyce as her "sister" in a letter to Lorde. Pat Parker Archives, Box 5, Schlesinger Library.

EUNSONG KIM is associate professor of English at Northeastern University and author of *gospel of regicide* and the forthcoming *The Aestheticization of Property: Race and the Politics of Collecting*.

Preface

When I was a child, eleven years old, I wrote my first story. It was published in the *SF Examiner*, and I was rewarded with a $2.00 check for my endeavors. Throughout my educational years the story, "How a Mascot Won the Baseball Game," would occasionally ping my creative juices; however, life is filled by those unexpected moments where the road veers right, but you careen left. And so it was that I fell in love with poetry and poets. For many years I toiled in those fields and it was fruitful. I loved the form. The euphony of cadence. The beautiful clarity of words floating on a page.

And then one evening (1982, possibly stoned), a post-dinner discussion, specifically about women's books, was whacked around like baseballs flying out of a batting cage. We were lamenting the lack of good contemporary lesbian fiction. We desired substance, plus engaging characters who were flawed and who would be able to survive an extraordinary situation. Fictitious? Why, yes! But framed within a plausible historical backdrop. Chaos. Friendship. Love. And karma. Were we asking for the moon? Raucous laughter! Matches flared. Cigarettes were lit. Coffee brewed. A voice (whose name I can't recall) from the middle of the table solemnly muttered, "the Bohemian Grove." Holy shit! All eyes shifted to the woman who had uttered those three words. Game on.

This was the Rubicon. Alea iacta est. There would be no retreat. I was a poet wading into uncharted waters. Could I answer the bell? Slowly, very slowly, I formulated the plot. Contemporary western. Lesbians. A Korean character. The Vietnam War. The Bohemian Grove. And, god help me, a talking German shepherd. Did I need more? Yes. The State of California. I'm a child of the sixties. I needed the familiarity of the region with all its innate wonder, craziness, and joie de vivre to cradle this book together. The only dodgy mishap: I lost sixty pages of the first draft through some computer glitch, and in the middle of the night drove my device to a couple of geeks who tried to recover the info but failed. Fortunately I had hard copy of the pages and feverishly transcribed everything back onto the computer.

Dancer Dawkins and the California Kid was published in May 1985 by Alyson Publications. I was thirty-nine. I had written a book while holding a forty-hour-a-week job, which, by the way, was the greatest employment I've ever had in my checkered career. The job literally saved my bacon. In retrospect, when I think of Dancer and the Kid, I marvel at my energetic youthfulness. My pluckiness. I had no Red Bull or drugs (loose lips sink ships) to push me across the finish line. I composed in a shotgun closet with my computer on top of a built-in chest of drawers. A small window that I faced reflected light during the day. And when it was time to pony up, Sasha

Alyson backed me again and published *Dead Heat*, a second book that featured Dancer, the Kid, Ta Jan, Killer Shep, and a new passel of characters.

Tempus fugit. Strange things happen when you cash in your chips for retirement. One day it's Sunday, and the next day is a blank. You don't know what day it is. And you don't care. Years lapse. Covid 1 along with iterations 2, 3, and 4 arrive. Lockdown? No problem. Solitary confinement? And masks? Sign me up! My elusive, covert nature relished the challenge. Then one day in my seventh-sixth year, I received a call from Shawn Wong, a University of Washington professor. Shawn, noted author, editor, and pioneer of six Asian American anthologies, is the founder of a series at UW Press that reissues notable works by Asian American authors. Shawn's proposal to me was a republication of *Dancer Dawkins and the California Kid*. I was stunned. Jesus H. I pondered his message over and over again. Resurrecting Dancer and the Gang! A resuscitation! Life after a thirty-eight-year Van Winkle nap on a dusty bookshelf.

"What's not to like?" Dancer replied.

"We've always been here for you," chimed in the Kid, the best wingman on the planet.

"And, you're the Gdamn OG! Bring on those props," they continued. "The book has legs!" And so it does.

Willyce Kim

DANCER DAWKINS
AND THE CALIFORNIA KID

BRICKS AND MISSILES

In a land sprinkled with an assortment of hills, the school sat perched on the highest peak in the city. On a clear day, fingers on the hands of passing strangers would point to the buildings in awe. What is it? they would ask.

Dancer Dawkins would usually answer: a cracker factory.

When the buildings were being constructed, many jokes were made. Such as: Why bother building on a hill of sand? Everyone knew that when the first great shaker came things were going to happen. Like flying bricks and wooden missiles. Like butter piled on a baked potato, the school was in for a long slide down. The nuns who were going to live there nodded, rattled their beads, and smiled. The carpenters, always high on something, crossed themselves and smiled back.

So it went. Two euphoric years of construction.

This was the time before California sinsemilla and the coming of Dancer Dawkins.

DANCER'S NAME

The first time Dancer Dawkins saw a football was on a June day when the temperature cracked 100 degrees. Sweat beading along the rim of her glasses, bare feet skimming blades of swooning bluegrass, Dancer was flying, was a blur, was a hot mirage of action as her hands plucked the piece of leather from the sky. "I think I have a problem," she said, when she saw the two defenders in front of her. "I think they're going to make a ham sandwich out of me," she said again, when she saw them part down the middle leaving her a pathway that even a pencil wouldn't poke through. Dancer slipped the football under her armpit and veered right.

The two defenders shifted with her.

She swiveled her hips left. The defender closest to her went with the rhythm of her body.

Dancer laughed. For an instant her body hung left. For an instant the two defenders were caught up in that motion.

Three leaning towers.

With one sweeping bladelike move Dancer cut right and was gone.

In those days after a touchdown no one spiked footballs. So Dancer just spit on the ground, wiped off her face, cleaned her glasses and said: "Gimme a cream soda." She felt magnificent. Now she knew why her parents named her Dancer.

THE DREAM

Once many years ago Dancer had this dream. She was walking along the beach carrying her fishing pole. The sky met the ocean in a splash of blue. There was no sound. No lapping of waves. No birds diving in and out of each other's cries. Nothing. Dancer found a cluster of rocks on which to stand and cast her line out. An hour. Two hours passed. Dancer was nodding off when she felt a hand on her shoulder. Mumbling something under her breath, Dancer slowly turned around. Three women stood in front of her without a stitch of clothing on. Dancer closed her eyes and opened them again. They were still there. One of them took her hand and led her away from the beach. The other two followed closely behind. As they walked, Dancer's clothes started to drop off and disappear. Dancer looked down and saw her right nipple harden. Oh shit, she mouthed. But it was already too late for that.

Dancer remembered her dream in the morning. In fact, she never forgot *that* dream. Every time she recalled certain details Dancer noticed a change in her breathing. Short driving spurts of air would emerge from her lungs, and her heart would be dipsy-doodling somewhere in her chest.

WOWIE-ZOWIE

While Dancer Dawkins was busy juking down a football field, Little Willy Gutherie was trying to stuff her sixth piece of Rubbles Dubble bubble gum into the already bulging corner pocket of her left cheek. Two months ago Willy had tried chewing tobacco. The tobacco made it. Willy didn't. Some friends had found Willy leaning over one of Whitehall Amusement Park's railings looking very green and very limp. A tiny stream of brown juice dribbled down Willy's chin. Before anyone could say wowie-zowie Little Willy Gutherie flashed the five knuckles of her right fist. No one ever mentioned chewing tobacco to Willy Gutherie again.

THE CALIFORNIA KID

For as long as there were full hot yellow moons and buckets of stars dotting up summer skies, for as long as the berries on Pine Hill had resembled thick ruby nuggets, maybe even longer than all that, she was always Little Willy Gutherie.

Never Gutherie. Sometimes Willy Gutherie. But most of

the time, "Little Willy Gutherie" rolled off tongues faster than cascading sparks from a dangling tailpipe.

The truth of the matter was Willy Gutherie was not little. She was not big either. Willy Gutherie likened herself to one of those electric blue dragonflies that were always buzzing over her favorite swimming holes.

One night Little Willy Gutherie caught the last half of a grade-B western. Someone was dying:

"Well, pardner, I guess I'm not going to make it."

"Nope. Guess we'll have to make it for you."

"Say, Arizona, how come if you never been to Arizona you got a name like that? . . ."

"Well, pardner—*gasp*—I always wanted to go there."

Clunk.

Little Willy Gutherie walked out of the room and crammed four pieces of Rubbles Dubble into her mouth. It took her two hours to pack her duffel bag and one minute to change her name to the California Kid.

Where was she going? To California, naturally.

SCRIBBLES

Dancer Dawkins was born accidentally . . . a genuine miscalculated rhythm-method child . . . on November 5 somewhere outside of Los Angeles. When she was twelve she lost her cherry while riding a horse named Tinker.

The California Kid was born and raised in Bangor, Maine. It has been rumored that her first words were "bow-wow." Unlike Dancer Dawkins, the Kid had never even put her butt in a western saddle until she was sixteen.

Dancer Dawkins, a double Scorpio, was heading up the California coastline via Highway One.

The California Kid, having crossed the Rocky Mountains, was lickety-splitting it for the land of giant artichokes and golden sunshine.

Their collision course was set.

ABSENT

Dancer spelled relief r-o-l-l-i-n-g. And that's exactly what she 5 was doing. While clipping along at a comfortable sixty miles an hour Dancer was busily manufacturing a joint with her right hand. This was not an easy task. Perfection was achieved through practice. Many hundreds of hours and many thousands of sheets of wheat straws did not go up in smoke. They went straight down the toilet . . . until Dancer's nimble fingers could coax and caress and roll right and left the finest of sun-cured flower tops.

A long lick, a fleeting look, and a quick light left Dancer tingling. The first toke exploded in a profusion of sage, scrub, and pulsating Humboldt County fields; hundreds of sun-kissed resins rat-a-tat-tatted across Dancer's tastebuds, parade right, they closed ranks and goose-stepped through her pearly gates. Upstairs. No one was home.

Gloriously cooked, Dancer's mind meandered right.

The highway faded left.

Just past San Luis Obispo her pulse quickened, and her heart flip-flopped one hundred times.

Jessica.

LOLO

Jessica Nahale Riggins. Product of a back-seat quickie in a '49 Ford, raised near the Kona Coast on the Big Island of Hawaii, migrated eastward to experience the Atlantic Ocean. Her parents wrote her off as "lolo," crazy. Nevertheless, whenever the good fortune of work had occasion to visit her, Jessica always wired money home. She was a good responsible girl; she was, and this is when Dancer's heart flip-flopped, green-eyed and tawny; a splash of sloe gin settling on the rocks; she was Dancer's "Nahale," her forest, two months gone to San Francisco and up to her tits in . . . what? Salvation?

Dancer's smile melted off into the sunset. Her foot floored the accelerator as last night's phone conversation rattled around in her memory bank.

Dancer grimaced. Jessica's parents were as right as rain. Jessica is "lolo." Which makes me "lolo" because I'm "lolo" over her.

SALVATION

Dancer had just finished a superb meal of spaghetti squash stuffed with mushrooms, green peppers, and onions, smothered by a thick tomato sauce laced with cheddar, when the phone rang. She crossed her fingers hoping it wasn't Bucky; she owed Bucky money and wasn't in the mood to make excuses for her delinquency.

The familiar buzz of long distance welled in her ear as a voice murmured, "Sweetie?" Dancer walked the phone into the kitchen. Dessert had arrived, just in the nick of time.

"Hey honey," Dancer purred, "I was just thinking of dropping you a line. How's it going up north?"

"Fine. Just fine," replied Jessica as she prostrated herself on the living room floor. "Dancer."

"I'm right here."

"I've found salvation."

Dancer stifled a laugh. "Is this a cousin of Sal Mineo or a relative of salmonella?"

Jessica groaned. "Be serious, Dancer, and please listen to me. I've been shown the way to salvation."

Dancer got up from the kitchen table. She was hysterical with laughter and almost dropped the phone. "Jessie," she gasped, "did you drop acid today?"

Jessica shifted around on the floor. This was not proving to be a fruitful conversation. "Dancer, maybe I should write you a letter. We don't seem to be connecting, and this is important."

"OK. OK. I'll be serious. You be serious, too," sighed Dancer, who felt as if she were sitting in a dentist's chair wavering somewhere between dread and tranquility.

"Well," said Jessica, "I now know what I would like to do for the rest of my life. I'm committed to being an emissary for Violia Vincente and her Venerable Brigade."

Far away in the recessed cavity of her upper molar Dancer heard the menacing sound of a dentist's drill. "What is that, some kind of drum and bugle corps?" she snapped. "Two months. You leave L.A. You leave me. Is this a job, or what? You're not being very clear."

"And you're not even listening to me. I'm sooo happy."

"For god's sake, Jess, you sound like you had a handful of reds for dinner."

"That's it. *Finis*. *Pau-hana*. The end," sputtered the self-anointed emissary. "I'll write you a letter."

"No letters," growled Dancer. "I'm coming up."

"I don't know if you can. The Reverend Mother runs a tight ship, and he's in the process of readying himself for some Bohemian festival, so security is tighter than usual."

"The who?"

"The Reverend Mother. Fatin Satin Aspen, our leader. We call him that behind his back," the exasperated Jessica replied.

"Jesus H," Dancer swore, "you've been brainwashed."

"Good-bye Dancer," Jessica replied, severing the connection.

Dancer slammed the receiver down and hurled the phone against the wall. It was the third set in six months; she was three for six at the plate.

Jessica remained lying on the living room floor. She felt as if she had just been pulled through a knothole backwards; her neck muscles were in spasm. "Oh cripes," she swore, and pulled out her Lebanese hash pipe.

HOTCAKES

Dancer Dawkins and Jessica Riggins met over a plate of hotcakes.

HOME MOVIES

Dancer loved hotcakes. Buckwheat hotcakes smothered with sweet butter and pure maple syrup made her smile in all the right places. Once Dancer ate hotcakes five days in a row. A childhood friend, Bucky Benton, recorded those gastronomical moments with her family's movie camera. When Mrs. Benton developed the film and replayed what she thought was the local church bazaar at a gathering of the Daughters of Christianity, and viewed 350 frames of Dancer Dawkins leering out from a golden forest of buttered pancakes she bit her lip in silence; when Dancer dropped her pants and mooned the stacked kitchen table Mrs. Benton pulled the plug. Bucky was grounded for a month.

KALEIDOSCOPE

Bucky and Dancer grew up in a suburb south of Los Angeles. They were good middle-class children who graduated from the same high school and had no interest in furthering their education. Bucky's parents pleaded. Dancer's parents threatened.

"What will you give us?" asked the children.

"A ride straight to the moon," thundered the Dawkins.

"A swift kick in the pants," answered the Bentons, who were quickly changing their tune.

They chose a small private school in Los Angeles. Bucky transferred after her second year to an art institute back East. There she became involved in firing clay and throwing parties; her glazes surpassed the latter and she soon became the toast of her department. Bucky basked in the baking.

Meanwhile, Dancer dropped out after her junior year. Her parents hit the ceiling. Her mother made excuses. "You're pregnant," she said. Or, "You're enlisting in the WACS." Dancer ignored the insults and moved to a small town, Camarillo, which was somewhat famous for its avocado groves and mental institutions.

There, drifting like a clam without a high tide, Dancer

clerked at a donut shop, and moonlighted weekends picking strawberries in the fields surrounding the town. Sometimes longing for glittering night-lights and palm-lined streets Dancer sojourned to L.A., which was just over the hill. She took particular joy in the rich coffee coolers at Old World, and the bountiful pasta plates at Michele's. Los Angeles was special: Los Angeles was a kaleidoscope of pastels, chlorine pools, and taqueria stands; it was also the home of the Dodgers; the hub of the entertainment industry; the cocaine mecca of the West, and the banana peel on which Dancer slipped.

DIAMONDS

On a thick Southern California night when the moon hung like a quartered cantaloupe in an endlessly hazy sky, Dancer Dawkins attended the West Coast premiere of Bucky Benton's latest art show. Nervously adjusting her Panama, Dancer sauntered across the threshold; the room was choked with Hollywood types; Dancer grabbed a Perrier from a passing waiter and scanned the area for Bucky. A wild Hawaiian print shirt backed out of a nest of people; Bucky looked up and caught Dancer's eye. Dancer tapped the rim of her Panama. They could have cut diamonds with their smiles.

EMERALDS

When Bucky relocated in Los Angeles she invited Dancer to join her. Dancer did not hesitate. She had smoothed out some rough edges in Camarillo, and she was ready to return to the glitter capital of the West.

"I feel short-tempered and evil," sneered Bucky, running her hand through her tousled hair.

"The bath didn't help, then," replied Dancer, who was happily stirring up a bowl of her favorite batter.

"No," scowled Bucky.

Dancer tried to ignore Bucky's mood, which increasingly soured as the evening passed. Bucky had been a victim of insomnia all week, and now, tonight, three houseguests were expected. "Some friends of a friend I owed a favor to," she wailed. "I hope they don't expect me to turn somersaults. I'll be lucky if I can even find the front door."

Dancer threw her head back and roared. She loved to goad Bucky. "You can handle the pressure, Buck. Just think, three lovely Boston women who have never sampled the delights of our state. Never eaten a stuffed artichoke, or sopped up gravy with a piece of sourdough. Come on, Bucky, wake up. Take a cold shower. I have the feeling you're going to need it."

The buzzer rang.

Dancer could hear murmurs at the door. She was beginning to flip her second hotcake when a voice from the edge of the kitchen said, "Have you always had such a muscular right forearm?" Dancer's flapjack hung in mid-air. She turned and gazed into the most marvelous set of emerald eyes this side of Thailand.

"Nope," she said. "It was only after I seriously started to masturbate that I noticed a significant change in my forearm's molecular structure."

Emerald eyes crinkled her face in laughter. A brazen response deserved closer scrutiny. "I'm Jessica Riggins," she finally said.

"Dancer Dawkins," responded the distracted cook.

"You always eat pancakes this late at night?"

"I eat hotcakes whenever I can. They're a treat."

"So you cater to your whims, do you?" came the quick reply.

"I try," said Dancer as she started stacking pancakes. "How was your trip out here?"

"So-so. I've never been this far west on the mainland. And I'm not quite sure if I'm even going to like Los Angeles."

Dancer chortled. "L.A. is not for the faint of heart."

Jessica watched the stack grow; they resembled gambling chips at a Las Vegas casino. "How many of those are you going to make?" she asked.

"As much as the batter will allow. You want a couple?"

"I wanna fuck," Jessica boldly replied.

Dancer looked hastily around the room. Bucky's crystals were still intact. The sound she heard shattering was her heart; her appetite could wait.

When Bucky Benton came back to the kitchen she discovered a mountain of orphaned pancakes, a dish of melting butter, and an open back door.

Bucky decided the time had come to take a cold shower.

SKETCH 1: DANCER

From the doorway of Bucky's kitchen Jessica had stolen several moments to watch Dancer perform with her pancakes. It was like a parade. Not only was Jessica impressed with Dancer's forearm; Dancer's face handsome with sun smelled like mountains and ocean; sweet pine and salt spray. Her mouth brimmed over with mirth. Thin silver-rimmed glasses pressed against the cheeks and rode haphazardly across the nose bone.

The hair curled upwards from the shirt collar in short, loose waves and drifted like a sea of wild oat grass on a pleasant bare-bottomed day. Jessica's body began to tingle. She felt like a Girl Scout on her first wilderness expedition.

SKETCH 2: JESSICA

The ability to perceive an object or a group of images from the corner of the eye without turning the head is called lateral vision. Dancer had great lateral vision. While flipping her hotcakes she was also busy charting the lines and the bones, the hither and yon of Jessica Riggins. Standing in the doorway, hands chucked deep into her pants pocket, Jessica filled the archway. Her hair, a tea-colored meshing of coils and wire, exploded in a multitude of aimless directions. Mercifully, it was short. Dancer wondered if it had ever been long as she tiptoed down the ridge of Jessica's nose and dove head-first into those luscious Key-lime-pie eyes. Train whistles screamed. And thunder rolled. Dancer Dawkins was blissfully drowning.

BLENDING

Sometimes dialogue is like the ritual of tequila. A lick. A swig. And a chomp.

FEINTS AND JABS

"I'd love to give it a try . . . see what I can come up with. I'm just not acclimating to this city, Dancer. San Francisco may not even be the answer, but I'm wasting away here." Jessica's voice fell like a limp flower into dead air. She covered her forehead with the palm of her hand partly to avoid looking at Dancer, who was sitting across the table from her, and partly because she was tired of the conversation. She had the strange feeling she should have never left her Atlantic Ocean.

Dancer watched Jessica dip away from her. She had noted the mechanical flutter in Jessica's voice and knew that she was either tired or bored. Dancer looked down into her coffee cup. Curse Bucky Benton, she thought, at least I was happy bagging donuts in Camarillo. "How long have we been together?"

Jessica looked up and sighed. "Almost two months."

Dancer tossed her hands into the air. "Well, doesn't that mean anything?"

"Of course it does."

"Talk is cheap, Jessie. Tell you what. My asthma's been picking up lately. You stay here in Los Angeles. And I'll go."

Jessica was annoyed by Dancer's glibness. She leaned back into her chair. "I fail to see the humor in this. We all know your lungs are bad. You want to go? Go." Jessica cut herself off. Dancer pushed away from the table. Oh shit, mused Jessica. She's going to pace.

The veins in Dancer's neck were bunching against her skin like a sack of wild potatoes. Moving towards the stove she formed her words methodically. "Jessica, I'm sorry if I made light of your situation. It wasn't intentional. It was strictly reflex. You know...."

Here it comes, groaned Jessica.

Dancer whirled and punctuated the air with short jabs. "I'm worried about you, Jessie. I really am. You're showing every sign of becoming a marvelous anal retentive."

Jessica suppressed a giggle and ignored Dancer's stance. She gazed out the window to her left. A northern gust of wind rattled the smog across the valley. Layers of clouds were beginning to slide across the face of the sun. It's a conspiracy, she thought, all a conspiracy. She turned and faced Dancer. "You may be right," she said. "Will you miss me when I'm gone?"

"Will you miss us?" Dancer shot back.

Jessica smiled and nodded. She wrapped her arms around Dancer's waist and pulled her down to her lap.

Outside the first drops of rain splashed against the kitchen window.

15

SHUFFLING

If Dancer knew then what she felt now ... DOOM ... she might have been a trifle more cautious with Jessie. But she would never lay odds on it. As Bucky Benton once said, "Better to be loose as a goose than tight as a kite."

Shuffling those words across the skyline, Dancer roared into San Francisco. Her speedometer had broken somewhere between Half Moon Bay and Pacifica. She calculated that she was doing forty-five to fifty miles an hour. The cop two lanes over clocked her at sixty. The car that had just turned left onto Fell Street thought it was another high-speed chase out of Bullitt and shot after both of them.

FORMALITY

The California Kid's real name was Wilhelmina Jennings Gutherie, Wilhelmina Jennings after her maternal grandmother. The family name was a tradition which got traditionally misplaced in the first wee hours of the Kid's delivery. Her grandmother said it was her mother. Her mother swore it was her Aunt Ida. Whoever it was stuffed tradition before the Kid had warmed her second set of diapers. The name Wilhelmina Jennings didn't have a prayer. In fact, it was last uttered by the Gutheries' parish priest as he performed the rite of baptism. After that, in some magical cooing moment, Grandmother, Mother, or Aunt Ida renamed the Kid, who even then looked like the greatest bundle since sliced bread, Little Willy Gutherie.

ROAD TEST

When Little Willy Gutherie, a/k/a the California Kid, celebrated her fifteenth birthday she became simultaneously eligible for her driver's license and the right to join the ranks of the working class.

Being a bright and clever child, Little Willy opted for the former. For hours the Kid mentally practiced the rudimentary fundamentals of stick-shift driving. When Mr. Gutherie took the Kid on a road test he was surprised by the Kid's dexterity. Hand and foot coordination flowed together in a stream of fluid motions.

Mr. Gutherie lit a cigar. He rolled the window down and remembered the day Little Willy crashed her bike into the retaining wall near Whitehall's park; bruised and dazed she kept mumbling, "Not enough lean, not enough lean."

Lean what?

Lean meat?

Lean to?

Mr. Gutherie flicked ashes out the window and was lost behind a layer of smoke.

The Kid glanced over at her ol' man. Her eyes were watering. She wished she had a Havana cigar too.

CRUISING

Propped up behind the wheel by two sets of pillows, the Kid felt a sense of power. She could leave her family and her friends and melt into a world of country backroads or four-lane city streets. Dreams and adventures came to rest on Little Willy's dashboard, and like chunks of brightly colored glass they illuminated those slow adolescent nights.

NUMBERED

Two weeks after Little Willy had slipped her driver's license into the plastic lining of her wallet, Mrs. Gutherie tried to have a summit conference with the Kid. Not known to be a woman of many words, Mrs. Gutherie cleared her plate and then cleared her throat. It was 8:30 a.m. and already seventy degrees out. Breakfast was almost finished. "You're fifteen," the mother began. "Mmm mmm," the Kid answered. She was busy scraping egg yolk off her dish with a wedge of toast, and her mouth was full.

Mrs. Gutherie began to wish she hadn't stopped smoking ten years ago. She always wished this after a particularly good meal. Over the years this added up to a lot of wishes.

Little Willy was pouring herself some coffee. Mrs. Gutherie watched her and sighed. "Hey, how many times do I have to repeat myself? Enough coffee. That's enough."

The Kid kept pouring. Picking up the container of cream she plucked the cap off with her teeth.

Mrs. Gutherie continued sighing.

Little Willy was getting nervous. She looked at her mother.

Mrs. Gutherie was drumming her fingers along the arm of her chair. She was a handsome woman. When she was younger her most ardent admirers referred to her as "Belle." Little Willy did not resemble her mother. She was the spitting image of her father, who came from hearty New England stock.

"What are you going to do today?" the older woman asked.

"Don't know," was the Kid's reply.

"Just remember," Mrs. Gutherie said as she gathered up the dishes, "idle hands are the devil's workshop."

"And all work and no play makes Jack a nut," Little Willy mumbled.

Before her mother could grab her, Little Willy scrambled out the back door. Skipping rocks over Duggan's pond, Little Willy knew her days were numbered.

CHECKERS

Luck. You're either born with it or you ain't. And Little Willy found that she had the luck of leprechauns coursing through her veins. Jobs, like fallen leaves, collected in piles around her shuffling feet. Dish washer. Movie usher. Library assistant. By the time she had graduated from high school Little Willy had a very checkered career.

BEANS

With a wad of Rubbles Dubble perched in her cheek, Little Willy stood behind the counter of Roxie's Malt Shop. Of all the jobs that the Kid would remember, nothing compared to the months that she spent pulling soda knobs, plumping ice cream onto cones, ladling rivers of hot fudge into sundae dishes, and flashing her famous (no cavities) teeth at anyone who ordered vanilla ice cream.

Good ice cream was becoming as hard to find as a five-cent cup of coffee. And good vanilla ice cream was slowly going the way of horse and buggy, and passenger train.

Dismayed but not discouraged, Little Willy became preoccupied with the quality of ice cream. Her rating system consisted of sight (texture, color, drip factor) and taste (real egg yolks, cream and milk). And vanilla. The prized bean spurred her towards the pinnacle of frozen foods. She pushed her taste buds relentlessly, weeding out the frauds one by one. She licked more, enjoyed less. She cultivated her disdain for sugar cones and stuck with the more conventional cake cones. She refused wooden spoons because they marred the flavor and reminded her of tongue blades at the doctor's office. In five months she threw up only once, gained a full and glorious ten pounds, and met her palate's pleasure at Roxie's.

ROXIE

Roxie Austin was twenty-eight. She had been making ice cream for five years, and eating it since she was three. She came from a long line of New England ice cream makers. It was rumored that her great-great-grandmother invented blueberry ice cream. This was partially true. One afternoon in a fit of rage the late Mrs. Austin hurled a pint of blueberries across the room. She was specifically aiming for her husband's large bony head. He ducked. She missed. Half the berries landed in a tub of vanilla ice cream. The rest was history.

When Little Willy Gutherie walked into her shop and ordered a vanilla ice cream cone, Roxie Austin cracked a smile as wide as the Grand Canyon. "Don't get too many customers that want just plain vanilla," she said, flipping up the freezer chest top. Roxie bent down. Little Willy watched her carefully. Roxie's forearm looked like a plank of soft pine; a platoon of muscles tap-danced along the inner ridge of her arm as she swiftly worked the ice cream back and forth into the bulging scooper. Little Willy was impressed. "You're pretty good with that," she said admiringly.

Roxie looked up and gingerly took a step back. "Say, what's the matter with your face? The mumps?"

Little Willy laughed and removed her wad. "Habit," she sheepishly replied.

Roxie squinted at the Kid and handed her the cone. Little Willy took a lick which was quickly followed by another. Then she took a bite. "Holy, holy, holy," the Kid whispered. Tears formed. Her tongue was coated with flecks of vanilla bean. "This is it," she exclaimed. "Absolutely," a neat swipe around the cone, "it."

Roxie Austin sat back on her stool behind the counter. She knew that this was serious business. She looked at the pink wad of gum balled up on Little Willy's wrist and she tried to focus on the black and white stripes of Little Willy's overalls.

She shook her head when she noticed Little Willy's golf cap. Then Roxie Austin locked onto Little Willy's pale blue eyes. If all was not lost before, all became lost now. Paler than a Texas bluebonnet. Brighter than a prairie-soaked sky. Roxie slowly inhaled. She could have sworn she saw the Kid's left eye twinkle.

Clearing her throat, Roxie interrupted, "Ah, if I didn't know any better I'd think you were in the middle of having an, uh . . ."

"I am," came the casual reply.

Clasping her hands around her right knee to keep from crashing off the stool, Roxie Austin recognized the chemistry of the moment. "Indeed. Indeed. This is an event. Are you always this eventful?" Not pausing for an answer Roxie decided to pull out all the stops. "How'd you like to work in this shop?"

Little Willy, who was polishing off the last bit of her cone, nearly choked. Weighing the pros and cons was pure formality. There were more pros and hardly any cons and infinite possibilities. The wheel of fortune slowly descended above Little Willy's head. Looking over at Roxie Austin she coyly uttered, "Only if you teach me how to make vanilla ice cream."

Roxie bit her tongue. What she was about to say she filed under future reference. What she did say was, "Vanilla ice cream!! Why kid," her right hand slapped the counter as she swayed heavily from the stool, "by the time you leave here you'll be a certified soda jerker; you'll know more about cones, sundaes, malts, sodas, and splits than my great-grandmother, I swear." Roxie grabbed Little Willy's hand. It felt like a cold fish. "Are you with me?" Little Willy's hand snapped back to life; she gave Roxie five.

FUTURE REFERENCE

Many months later on a slow afternoon, Little Willy Gutherie's head bobbed up and down like fishing float. Her hair adrift in a sea of thighs she was marking time for Roxie Austin, who . . . ohhh sweet mama . . . waves of crushed vanilla beans.

LOGISTICS

On the fateful evening that Little Willy Gutherie changed her name to the California Kid, Jessica Riggins was settling down to a fitful night's sleep in San Francisco; Dancer Dawkins was trying to glue herself back together again; Bucky Benton was stretching canvas in Burbank; and Roxie Austin had just celebrated her thirty-fifth birthday.

A calculating creature, Willy Gutherie was stunned by the speed of her own actions. Packed in less time than it took to watch a Sunday matinee, the Kid felt like a silver-finned salmon rushing through uncharted waters looking for that familiar mountain stream.

All that remained of her when she left Bangor was carved on the trunk of an old birch tree. The inscription read: WG loves RA. She was eighteen then, and her summer passed like a cargo-laden banana boat slowly winding its way up the Amazon or down the Amazon depending on the logistics of the given moment.

HEIST

If her departure had been made on horseback, Little Willy Gutherie would have left clouds of dust billowing in her wake.

As it was, her parents did not fully comprehend the frenzied nature of her decision. Mrs. Gutherie sighed in disbelief.

"George," she began. Behind the folds of the Sunday paper came a muffled, "Mmmmmmm."

"George, will you put the sports section down and pay attention."

"In a minute, hon, just one more minute."

Belle grunted. If she had taken all of George's minutes and strung them back to back she'd have a brand new day. Sliding along the table, Belle reached across the dishes and pulled the paper from her husband. Then with a great show of flourish she folded the sporting green into a large triangle and sat on it.

"For god's sake, George, our only child has picked up and left for the West Coast, the kingdom of cults, fads, and sex, and all you're interested in is whether the Yankees picked up any ground on the Red Sox."

"Now just calm down, Belle. Let's remember that Willy has been on her own since she was seventeen."

"How can I forget that," sputtered the exasperated Belle. "She's twenty-four, and . . ."

"Twenty-five," chimed George.

"She's whatever," waved Belle, "gone to California. If she cared she would have stayed here."

"Belle, now you know that's not true. She lived here and we never saw her."

Nodding, Belle Gutherie threw up her hands in disgust. "I wish I had a carton of Chesterfields," she muttered.

Her husband glided into the living room and picked up a flat brass-hinged box. His fingers followed the grain of wood to the tiny clasp that gleamed like a gold nugget in the bottom of a prospector's pan. George licked his lips and lifted the lid. "Sons of bitches," he screamed. "I've been robbed. They're gone, all gone except for one." Lovingly holding the last of his private stock, Havana's finest, between his fingertips, George moaned, "Belle, *your* girl has taken me to the cleaners."

Belle Gutherie poured herself another cup of coffee. She added a slug of brandy and closed her eyes. Not only was her twenty-five year-old daughter descending upon California without her blessing, but she was also packing twelve priceless Havana cigars, the crown jewels of the Gutherie household.

Belle opened her eyes. Sobs drifted in from the living room. George had just lit his last Havana.

GREETINGS

The flickering lights of the patrol car had finally caught Dancer's attention. She tried not to hyperventilate as she stepped from the car.

"What's the problem, officer?" she wheezed.

Badge #2149 glanced down at Dancer and scowled. She looked like the wife that had left him and the daughter that never wrote home.

"This is a thirty-five mile an hour zone, lady. I clocked you at fifty minimum."

Dancer's heart thudded against her chest.

Badge #2149 droned on. He flipped Dancer's license back to her and tore the ticket from his book. "Welcome to San Francisco," he snarled.

Dancer bit her lower lip. A swarm of calculations filled her mind.

"Jesus Christ," she muttered. "I could have flown one way."

Crumpling up the ticket in her fist, she slid into the driver's seat and had a hit of Primatene Mist.

Her lungs cleared. She struggled to deep-breathe, but couldn't shake the feeling that she was being watched.

Off to her left, eucalyptus trees floated through the dark. Dancer removed her glasses and rubbed them against her shirt. Better. She thought. Better. Some of the night's sparkle returned as she pushed the frames back against her face.

Hungry, and suddenly very cold, Dancer envisioned oak logs crackling in fireplaces, and the smell of coffee wafting through the trees.

She shifted from side to side. Golden Gate Park was straight ahead. Of that she could be certain—which was much more than she could say for Jessica.

POTHOLES

Three cars back Little Willy Gutherie felt like a third wheel on a blind date. What was she doing chasing patrol cars? And where was she going? Little Willy stuffed another piece of gum into her mouth; she was quite accustomed to her life filling up with questions. Fortunately, unlike math, life's problems had various solutions, but the bulb of enlightenment did not dawn on Little Willy's muddled crown until after high school. The world, much to her relief, was not littered with numerical stumbling blocks, but riddled instead with philosophical potholes. Buoyed by this realization, Little Willy smugly patted her heart. Life was no longer a three and two count. The sun rose and the sun set on a brand-new ball game.

LEVI'S AND FLANNEL

When Dancer stepped from her car, Little Willy turned down her radio. Her fingers blindly tapped the steering wheel. There was an aura of familiarity and comfort radiating from Dancer's flannel shirt and Levi's. Little Willy scanned Dancer for more clues. Streetlights glinted off Dancer's frames. Little Willy slowly blew on her hands. She watched Dancer crumple up the ticket and crowed in silent admiration at her boldness. A growing sense of frustration tugged at Little Willy's shirtsleeves. Wanting a closer look at the person behind the silver-rimmed glasses, she decided to make her move.

SCRAMBLED EGGS

Dancer scratched a match across the dashboard and lit a joint. After the first two tokes her thoughts collapsed like a bowlful of scrambled eggs about to hit the frying pan. She didn't care which way the fat was flying.

Muttering something like, "Boy, I really needed that," Dancer searched for a hard rock station. She wanted to fill the car with heavy metal and pull away from the curb in style.

FIRECRACKERS

Sometimes the best of plans fizzle like a bag of wet firecrackers. A lot of smoke and hardly any action. Dancer cranked up the audio and smiled into the rear-view mirror. Her lids were at half-mast. The joint was jumping and it was time to go.

Dancer reached forward and turned the ignition over.

Nothing happened. Her car had made other plans for the evening.

EXPLORATION

Little Willy Gutherie edged out onto Fell Street. Her wheels were turning. She was tired, hungry, and curious; San Francisco pulsated with a big-city rhythm that beckoned her modest New England heart. She was desperate to explore all the nooks and possibly even some of the crannies. But for that she needed a guide.

Dancer's car loomed like a star on the horizon. Instinct drove Little Willy toward it. Her family motto, "Never a reckless adventure," flashed through her noggin. She reached for a cigar. If her father could only see her now.

FLOODED

Dancer was nearing the end of her rope. The night was slowly turning over on her. She had no patience. If she had more patience she would have less asthma, but such was not the case. And now her car was in the same state her mind was in: flooded. Dancer stared out the window. What she wanted most was a platter of buckwheat pancakes. And what she wanted after that was Jessica. Dancer's mouth tightened. She suddenly remembered her mission and the evening's mishaps. Steam clouded the windows. Dancer flung the door open.

HEADLINES

The Department of Motor Vehicles has stated that a car traveling at the rate of ten miles an hour can inflict considerable damage upon a stationary object. Little Willy had just dropped into second gear, bit the top off her Cubano, sunk back against the cushioned seat, when she ripped the door off Dancer's car. It was like the 5:10 blind-siding a stack of egg cartons. Little Willy's life passed in front of her. She saw her name in headlines. "I came to California for this!" she exclaimed. Little Willy's car came to a standstill. Her heart was doing the herky-jerky. Filled with more fear than loathing she gazed into her rear-view mirror. Dancer was still seated behind the steering wheel. Music blared into the street. Someone was having a party.

NIGHTMARE

Resting her forehead against the steering wheel, Dancer hopelessly tried to still the soundtrack of the accident, which now clattered endlessly like a record stuck on replay in the cavern of her quickly fading mind.

Music poured through the car. Shaking herself Dancer mumbled, "This is a fuckin' nightmare."

Running her hand along the dashboard, and patting all the knobs, she apologized to her car, Pirate Jenny.

Moving slowly, Dancer stepped through the gaping hole into the street.

BLACKJACK

At the precise moment Dancer stepped from her car, Little Willy Gutherie emerged from hers. The park across the street looked dark and foreboding; the stream of cars rushing east along Fell had slowed to a trickle.

Little Willy clapped her hands together, and sank them deep into her pants pockets.

"Why did I come West?" she asked herself as she gingerly approached Dancer.

"Why did I come to San Francisco?" jingled Dancer's mind.

"It's the pinched cigars," moaned Little Willy.

"It's my karma," cried Dancer, "and that fucking Jessica."

"What a pickle I'm in," shivered Little Willy.

"I'm all washed up," grimaced Dancer, whose breathing suddenly became highly erratic.

Little Willy stopped dead in her tracks. She felt like she was wearing lead boots. She looked down at her Fryes.

Then she glanced at Dancer.

Dancer's mind had begun to fade the minute the door left its hinges.

At ten feet, she took off her glasses and folded them neatly in her pocket.

At five feet and wheezing like an embattled marathon runner, Dancer took one last gasp and closed the distance between her and Little Willy.

Little Willy's mind was aflutter with one-line statements.

"Gee, I'm sorry" sounded good.

Or, "It happened so fast I didn't see you" sounded even better.

Unfortunately for her she didn't need to make excuses.

What she really needed was a hefty blackjack, because Dancer, whose lungs were in the highest state of anxiety, swiveled to the left, took one step back, and punched Little Willy's lights out.

ICY STARS

The first time Little Willy saw stars was not through a telescope. Perched like a bantam on a strawberry roan, urged on by her Cousin Ted's forty-dollar wager, and amply fortified by a country breakfast of eggs, hash browns, and slabs of Virginia bacon, Little Willy threw caution to the winds and heaved her saddle to the ground.

The bright morning sun made Little Willy squint; she loved the chill of autumn in the crisp New England air, the tang of fall apples, and pumpkins baking in spicy pies; she also loved a good bet.

Little Willy walked her horse around the course. A glimmer of fear slid across her palms. She had never jumped bareback, but a Smith and Wesson folding knife beckoned from L.L. Bean's catalog, and determined to place the carrot before the horse, she buried her anxieties in the wealth of her forthcoming rewards.

"This is going to be a cinch," she thought as her horse hit a trot.

"One flannel shirt, two pairs of socks, and a Smith and Wesson pocketknife," she crowed as the horse swung into a canter.

"Dinner for two at Aldo's," she chortled as the big roan soared through the air.

"A hospital bed and a body cast," she screamed as she felt herself slipping from the leaping horse.

Little Willy's body flipped once in mid-air before crashing to earth. Her head reeled from the initial impact. Clouds of light hurtled before her eyes, exploding in a shower of blinding color.

"Ice," she muttered.

Her cousin peered down at her. He shook his head; sure as shit he wouldn't risk life and limb for a mere forty dollars. And what was it she was trying to say before passing out? "Ice and stars"?

Cousin Ted scratched his head.

Had he bothered to listen he would have distinctly heard Little Willy exclaim, "I see stars."

SHRINE

Dancer watched Little Willy's body slump against the side of a parked car. The car acted as a wedge, momentarily propping up Little Willy.

Dancer rubbed the knuckles of her hand and slipped her glasses back on.

Little Willy let out a moan and tried to regain her footing. She felt like she was skidding across the deck of a small boat. Her legs buckled under her as the street heaved to and fro. A thin trickle of blood seeped out of Little Willy's mouth; half-heartedly, she tried to grope her way through the fog bank which engulfed her. Slowly she rolled her tongue over her perfect no-cavities teeth. Satisfied that she wasn't going to wake with a mouthful of Chiclets, and convinced that the evening was a nightmare, Little Willy flicked her head back, saw the stars turning over head, and crumpled to the ground.

Dancer caught Little Willy before her head hit the pavement.

"She's dead and I'm holding the bag," Dancer thought as she reminded herself over and over again not to panic, to act like a rational adult, and to ignore the wheezing sounds pouring from her chest.

The refrain "whymewhymewhymewhyme" circled through Dancer's mind like a flock of vultures looking for a place to land.

"I promise to never smoke again and to have a shrine built on this very spot," Dancer gasped as she pulled Little Willy to the curb, and anxiously searched for a pulse.

REVIVAL

Cradling Little Willy's head in her lap, Dancer gazed down the length of Little Willy's body. Cuffed Levi's rode lazily over a pair of worn boots. A pale blue chamois shirt poked through Little Willy's jacket which rubbed softly against Dancer's hand as she loosened bits and pieces of clothing.

Dancer placed her fingers along the side of Little Willy's neck.

Little Willy smiled. She was dreaming of Roxie and her big square hands.

Dancer drew her hand away when Little Willy smiled. "There must be life after death," she thought.

Little Willy groaned.

Dancer's heart jumped. She wished she had a capsule of

smelling salts. Then she could break it under Little Willy's nose and be off the hook.

Dancer stared off into the park. Fortunately, she had a good memory which compensated for her over-active mind. A flurry of still-life scenes bombarded her senses. She remembered high school P.E. and the night she hit the deck during a basketball game.

Cupping Little Willy's chin in her hand Dancer softly cried, "Hey."

Little Willy dreamed on.

Dancer shook her gently and cried, "Hey," again.

A low moan escaped from Little Willy's lips. Dancer jumped on it the way a drowning person dives in for a lifesaver.

"What city are you in?" pleaded Dancer. "What city are you in?" she repeated again.

Little Willy's lips pushed the words out. She had no idea where she was. Her gray matter was on vacation somewhere in the Rocky Mountains. Chaos momentarily reigned.

"Fort Sumner," she murmured.

"Fort Sumner? Fort Sumner what?" echoed the startled Dancer.

"New Mexico."

"Fort Sumner, New Mexico," Dancer echoed again. She licked her lips. The situation was bordering on critical.

Crossing her fingers, Dancer asked, "Your name . . . what is your name?"

A glimmer of a smile burrowed its way from Little Willy's heart and slid across her bloodied lip.

"Kid," she haltingly replied. "California Kid."

"The California Kid?"

"Fort Sumner, New Mexico?"

"Holy shit," Dancer screamed, "brain damage," and almost dropped the Kid.

The Kid's eyes flicked open. "Close, but no cigar," she whispered.

HATCHING

Dancer slapped her thigh and stamped her foot. Gusts of nervous laughter flew from her raised head and darted through the Panhandle like a cluster of hummingbirds on a late-night binge.

"You know," Dancer said, "I thought a minute ago, haha, you were almost six feet under and ready to push up some daisies."

The Kid, whose head was throbbing, groaned. Her lip felt like it needed a trayful of ice. She peered up at a semi-hysterical Dancer, who was counting her blessings. Bracing herself, she slowly rose off the curb.

"That was some Sunday punch," the Kid exclaimed as she dusted off her clothes and rotated her neck and shoulder muscles.

Dancer noted the swelling in the Kid's lip. Remorse filled her heart. "At least it's not murder one," she gulped.

The Kid glanced over at Dancer. Various solutions to their predicament had hatched while she was stretching.

"I bet you think I'm going to humor you," the Kid said as she ran her hand along the pinstripes of a parked Mustang.

"Umm, fat chance," interrupted Dancer. "The wool," she continued, "has not been pulled over my eyes since . . ." and here Dancer's voice faded down the homestretch, ". . . since Jessica," her heart stormed. "Since imitation maple syrup," she heard herself say.

"Well, let's skip the preliminaries, and get onto the main event." The Kid fired straight from the hip. "The way I see all of this is you sucker-punched me. I'll drop the assault and battery charges if we can work an amicable settlement over your car."

Dancer rubbed her forehead and wiped her glasses with a bandana. She was bristling with indignation.

The Kid fidgeted with her jacket zipper.

"What kind of money are you talking about?" Dancer asked.

"None to begin with," the Kid slowly answered, taking a step back, and carefully scrutinizing Dancer.

The veins in Dancer's neck pounded against her skin. "You got a lot of nerve," she shouted. "But the hard cold fact is this: I don't have a car door. And without a car door, I have no car. I'm here from L.A. on business, and I need those wheels. Got the picture, Kid?"

The Kid noticed Dancer's shortness of breath. "I'll tell you what," she hastily said. "I'll make you an offer you can't refuse."

"You better give it your best shot, Kid."

"I'll help you lash your door back on so it will be securely parked along this street. Then I'll chauffeur you any place you so desire providing we get along better than we have tonight."

Dancer mulled over the Kid's words for ten seconds. "That's it?" she yelled.

The Kid nodded, and took another step back.

Dancer shook her head, and studied the Kid's face. She couldn't see a better offer coming down the road, and bargaining was not one of her strong suits. Shrugging her shoulders, she stiffly offered up her palm.

The Kid bravely smiled through her upper lip and clasped Dancer's hand. "Done," she said.

"You know, Kid, you're quite a little hustler."

The Kid turned away and looked off into the distance. Her eyes twinkled with laughter; there wasn't a speck of truth in what Dancer had just said.

SARDINES

Lashing the car door to the main body of the car was easier than expected. The Kid supplied the nylon cord and Dancer the finesse; they strapped the door, a metallic sheet curled at the fringes like a sardine top, against the steering wheel, and the side bar of the rear window.

Satisfied that Pirate Jenny was anchored securely, Dancer collected her duffel bag and assorted asthmatic paraphernalia. Tossing her baggage into the Kid's car and looking back at Jenny forlornly, Dancer hoped the moon was in Scorpio. If the moon was in Scorpio she could reason away her sudden rash of bad luck. If not, shit creek was starting to resemble the Pacific Ocean.

GOOSE

The Kid and Dancer drove around looking for an all-night eatery. They made a left down Masonic and a right on Haight. Tiny knots of street people gathered on corners, or clustered in doorways. Shopfronts gleamed in the cool reflective night lights.

Dancer looked glumly past the rows of closed stores.

"There's not one damn restaurant open," she swore. "If only we were in L.A.," she wistfully continued, "there wouldn't be this problem."

The Kid nodded wisely in agreement. She had never been to L.A., but she thought that in this moment of frustration her affirmation would somehow lighten the hunger pangs that were threatening to short-circuit their conscious minds.

"I'm starving," the Kid exclaimed. "I'd like a steaming cup of coffee, baked potato, no sour cream, hold the chives, fillet of sole, French-cut string beans, and a huge scoop of vanilla ice cream."

Dancer fell face-forward against the dashboard in mock amazement.

"Make a left, make a left, make a left," she cried.

The Kid swung up Stanyan Street.

"What's that?" screamed Dancer.

The car jerked to a halt. There, recessed among the brick and cobblestone, nestled like a hen bedded down in straw, was a twenty-four-hour diner aptly called the Golden Goose.

THE GOLDEN GOOSE

The Kid and Dancer hopped from the car. They swept past the warm glow of lights emanating from the restaurant windows and burst through the front door the way a crest of water floods the beach.

"Holy shit," said the Kid.

"I don't believe it," whispered Dancer as she backed into the door and swiveled her head around.

There, snugly lining one wall and dovetailing into the next, were five wooden booths all dimly lit by white and gold goose-shaped lamps; covering each table was a Dutch blue batik depicting a flock of geese sweeping over a pond in flight. Overhead, a webbing of miniature Christmas tree lights adorned the ceiling. Against the back wall behind the counter hung a three-foot walnut-framed portrait of the biggest goose of them all: Mother. In front of that and to the side rested a golden egg-shaped cash register, and standing behind it was a middle-aged Asian woman drinking a large cup of coffee.

She stared at the two women and shook her head. Brother, were they a mess. One of them had a swollen lip and the other had lint all over her glasses. She looked at her wristwatch. It was two-thirty in the morning.

"Ahem," said the woman.

Dancer nudged the Kid.

"Do you plan to stand there all night or would you like some food?"

The Kid and Dancer sheepishly glanced at each other and wandered over to a booth. Their hostess placed two huge steaming mugs of coffee and a cream-spouting goose in the middle of the table and disappeared behind an ornate swinging door.

The Kid handed Dancer a menu and smiled.

Together they opened their menus and read the following message:

Welcome to the Golden Goose
Our motto is: Fresh is best
If you don't see it, ask.
Our hours are from noon to three a.m.

We are open every day of the year except
Monday night during football season.
Bon appétit, the Korean.

"Whew," Dancer exclaimed.

"That was just the tip of the iceberg," the Kid said, flipping the page as she watched Dancer's jaw drop like a medieval drawbridge across the festive table.

Their senses were visually bombarded. Food entrees popped up like mushrooms in a rain-soaked cow field. Omelets were followed by hors d'oeuvres; desserts cavorted with sandwiches; salads bloomed among the curries.

Dishes brandished names like:

The Mae West Preserver: bagels floating in a sea of lox, cream cheese, and red onion rings.

The Fonda Fixeggtion: a mushroom, avocado, jack cheese omelet wedded to half a grapefruit, and twenty jumping jacks.

The Liliuokalani Cooler: Royal pineapple juice, fresh coconut milk, and a scoop of vanilla ice cream.

The Navratilova Dropshot: splash of grenadine on the rocks, soda back with lime.

The Gertrude Stein-off: two fudge brownies and a warm glass of milk.

"I'll take one of each," cried Dancer.

"Bring on the food," chorused the Kid.

But they may as well have been camping out in the Mojave Desert, or experiencing springtime in the Rockies, because their voices bounced off the walls like sounds ricocheting down wilderness trails.

Civilization was to the right, behind the swinging door.

SUBMISSIVE

Dancer drained her coffee cup, slid from the booth, and went in search of their hostess. The big toe of her right foot had just crossed the plain of the back counter when a low growling chilled her warm, caffeinated heart. Dancer slowly twisted her head and locked eyes with a snarling German shepherd.

"Help," she weakly cried.

The Kid rushed from the booth.

"For cripe's sake," pleaded Dancer, "not so fast."

The Kid broke into a walk, and tiptoed towards the counter.

The shepherd took one step forward.

Dancer averted her eyes submissively and retreated half a step.

The Kid, glimpsing the shepherd's raised lips and deeming the situation serious but not critical, propelled herself several steps backwards.

The hostess, who had reappeared through the swinging door wearing a Walkman headset, took one look at the absurd tableau and snapped her fingers.

The shepherd trotted over to her side.

Dancer patted the counter weakly and said, "Good dog."

The hostess looked over at Dancer. At least this one was better than the last one, who knew nothing about dogs and their pecking orders. The poor fool. The last one had peed in her pants.

THE KOREAN

The Korean's baptismal name was Penelope Frances Lee. This never pleased her. Neither did living on the island of Oahu. Sometimes, after school, she'd sit under a coconut tree dipping green mangoes into soy sauce, fantasizing about cattle and snow and the big cold sky of Montana.

This was years before the vegetarian movement, and the beginning of her cowboy phase.

Her sister often found her cooling off in the house basement smoking pilfered cigarettes.

"Please don't tell Mom, please don't tell Mom," became one of her more rhythmical refrains.

The other, "Whadcha call me Penelope for?" unlocked entire chorus lines.

"The real Penelope was a dud."

"She was a queen," her mother would answer.

"A dud."

"A queen."

"Some queen. All she ever did was weave, weave, weave. Jeez-louise, Penelope just sucks."

Her mother, never believing in the old "wait till your father gets home" adage, would reach for the leather.

The Korean would reach for the front door knob.

As the Korean got older she became wiser, and in her wisdom she learned to yell such profundities from behind the safety of a locked bedroom door.

MIGRATIONS

In 1903 the SS *Gaelic*, carrying the first boatload of Korean plantation workers from Inchon Harbor, arrived in the Hawaiian Islands.

Between 1910 and 1925 the second wave, largely comprised of Korean picture brides, continued the influx of migrant laborers.

In 1967, approximately sixty years after the immigration

of her grandparents and four months before the infamous "Summer of Love," Penelope Frances Lee waved aloha to the island of Oahu and crossed the Pacific Ocean with a suitcase full of Thai sticks.

San Franciscans opened their golden gates.

She unlatched her suitcase.

The Yellow Pearl had struck gold, and the rest, as they say, was history.

In 1968 the Haight buried the hippie. Burned-out street urchins consumed cans of Alpo while fingering their love beads.

Penelope Frances Lee, disinherited daughter of the mayor of Honolulu, merchant emeritus of the Haight, honorary godmother to scores of aspiring tribal children, never looked back.

In 1969 she emerged from a phone booth as Ta Jan the Korean.

KILLER SHEP

"That was a helluva close call," wheezed a grateful Dancer.

"Yeah, lucky for us," chimed in the Kid.

The shepherd, recognizing small talk when she heard it, dropped to her master's side. Behind the air of obedient passivity the shepherd was yucking it up. She was nine years old and a bit arthritic. Entire portions of her day were spent in the back rooms of the restaurant. An episode like this relieved her boredom. She loved scaring the bejeezus out of unsuspecting customers, and these two were sitting ducks. The shepherd's eyelids were beginning to droop.

"Is he all bluff, or does he bite?" asked the starving Dancer, who at this point was straining to make meaningful conversation.

"She," emphasized their hostess, "has bitten many people. The stars were in your corner, and your weight is upon my egg."

Dancer looked blankly at the Kid. All her life she had wrestled with the meaning of poetry, the moral of the story, and detested it. Now, their hostess was speaking in riddles.

The Kid waded through Dancer's mind. "I think," she said, "you should remove your elbow from the cash register."

"Oh," murmured Dancer, straightening up.

"What is it you both wish?" ventured their patient hostess, who instinctively knew they both needed a warm meal and professional guidance. It did not take a genius to recognize these facts, but just for the record the Korean was a genius.

"Buckwheat pancakes," began Dancer. "And a glass of orange juice, and more of that delicious coffee."

"Fish," said the Kid. "You got any fish today?"

"Trout," replied the Korean.

"Trout, a baked potato, hold the sour cream and chives, the house vegetable, and a dish of vanilla ice cream."

The Korean nodded.

"By the way, your dog, what's her name?" asked Dancer.

"Killer Shep."

"Killer Shep!" the Kid and Dancer chorused.

From somewhere deep in canine dreamland, Killer Shep twitched and grinned. The Korean was full of it tonight. The only morsels Killer Shep had ever bitten were doggie biscuits and kitchen soup bones.

The Korean edged closer to the counter and felt Killer Shep stifling a laugh. She made a mental note to discuss this recurring ESP with her therapist. Tonight, however, good fortune brought her these two cookies.

"My name," she said ever so slowly, "is Ta Jan the Korean."

SLEIGHT-OF-HAND

"Ohh."

"Ahh."

Were the only sounds that filtered through "gooseland" as the Kid and Dancer put away their meal.

Sleight-of-hand, the Korean moved around them shuffling dishes to and fro like a grand wizard of the culinary knights.

Dancer wiped the corners of her mouth. "You sure know how to eat, Kid."

The Kid smiled down at her plate. Good cooking was like great art. And a square meal always took the edges off a hard day. "To the chef," she said, raising her water glass.

"To the chef," Dancer replied.

Killer Shep's ear perked up at the sound of clinking glasses. "Another great meal down the hatch," she rumbled.

Ta Jan, who was sandwiched between her Walkman and a current issue of *Rolling Stone*, gazed fixedly at the kitchen clock.

"It's time," she said. "They're teetering like two overstuffed peppers on the brink of a well-oiled baking dish." Placing their bill upon a platter, she marched through the swinging door.

AFTERMATH

Smoke rings fluttered through the restaurant like miniature rice-paper kites. The Kid tapped her cheek with her index finger and sent a steady stream of circles aloft. Tranquility hovered like halo plumes. A good meal deserved a good cigar, and the Kid happily supplied the best.

"I feel like a king. Do you feel like a king? I feel like a king," the Kid sighed.

"You're repeating yourself," smiled Dancer as she took a long puff off her cigar and squinted playfully across the way. "To tell you the truth, Kid, I shouldn't be indulging in this," confessed Dancer, waving her Cubano like a baton. "Bad lungs run in the family, and my asthma has been active lately."

"I'll say," thought the Kid as she gazed lovingly at her own cigar. "Is there something that would make it better?"

"Acupuncture," suggested a low voice from the rear. "The therapeutic merits of this Eastern medicine have been found to be quite beneficial. Relief for you," continued Ta Jan slowly, "may be just a few silver needles away."

Dancer scowled. Needles terrified her. The thought of injections always made her wheeze. "Thanks, but no thanks for your suggestion," she said. "I'm a little gun-shy of needles."

Ta Jan placed their bill upon the table. "Perhaps you will consider it later in life," she softly replied.

The Kid stubbed out her cigar. "That was the best meal I have eaten in two weeks. My compliments to the chef," she said, nodding to Ta Jan. "You wouldn't happen to know of—"

"Or could recommend," thought Dancer.

"Of a place to stay," finished the extrasensory Ta Jan, who slid in next to the astonished Kid.

"You took the words—"

"Right out of my mouth," mimicked Killer Shep, who was the first to recognize the low rumblings. Nervously padding over to Ta Jan she dropped to the floor and crept under the table.

"Well," continued Ta Jan, "perhaps you could stay at my place, but I suggest that for the moment we all follow Killer's example and heave ourselves under a table because an earth-quake is about to hit."

MUZZLE

"Oh shit," yelled the Kid as she slipped under the table and came eyeball to eyeball with Killer Shep. "Now listen, pal, we're in this together," panted the Kid, "so don't you give me a hard time."

"Anything you say," thought Killer Shep passively.

"And furthermore," continued the Kid, "I need some breathing room."

Killer Shep scooted over and tilted her head. The Kid's knees were knocking together; edging a bit closer she caught a whiff of "the dreads," fear spores that seep out of people when they are traumatized.

The Kid reached into her pocket and stuffed a chunk of gum into her mouth. She rolled it around for a while before gingerly cracking it between her teeth.

Killer Shep's lips parted in a smile. "This one shows a lot of promise," she thought.

The Kid glanced over at the Shep. "Wipe that smile off your muzzle," she ordered. "This is serious business."

Killer Shep nodded and winked. "Here's looking at you, Kid," she happily woofed.

KER-CHUNK

The earthquake was what native Californians called a "roller." Instead of a sharp jolt, rattle, jolt, the quake felt like a flat tire on a slow roll downhill. KER-CHUNK, THUD, THUD. KER-CHUNK, THUD, THUD. Dishes rattled. A few hearts jumped, then it was over.

Jessica, who was asleep, entered her third dream during the earthquake and didn't feel a shudder. Dancer, who was less than ten blocks away, took off her glasses and stood under a doorway. Jessica moaned into the sheets; her third dream was soaked in eroticism.

The Kid slowly put her hand on her chest and felt for her heart. Slowly she reached over and stroked Killer Shep's ears. "We made it, girl," she whispered. Together they crawled out from under the table.

Flushed and animated, Dancer and Ta Jan were sitting at the counter discussing the quakes of '69 and '74.

"How'd you hold up, Kid?" asked Dancer.

"And you, my little biscuit-breath?" queried Ta Jan.

"Is that all there was?" replied the Kid nonchalantly.

"Could have fooled me," nuzzled Killer Shep.

"Unfortunately for all of us, it may be just beginning," observed Ta Jan.

CATASTROPHE

Jessica woke when the morning bell rang and promptly jacked off. She did not remember her erotic dream, but her pillows lay suggestively between her legs. Always one to seize a ripe moment, Jessica fantasized about nuns and came.

Dressing slowly and savoring the solitude, Jessica reached for her indigo robes. Patting her left side, she touched her knife. All members were issued a standard five-inch blade.

Some wore them openly at the hip; Jessica preferred the edge of concealment.

Standing in front of the full-length mirror, Jessica studied herself for weaknesses. "Think tough, be tough, tough as nails," she muttered rapidly. Her final exams were scheduled for five o'clock. She held out her hands and searched her palms as if picking her way through an old creased map.

A long time ago an old *kahuna* had forecast that she would leave the Pacific to wade in the Atlantic and straddle California between her toes.

Jessica's Key-lime-pie eyes glittered like dewdrops on a blade of grass. Smoothing her robes, she stepped back against the wall. As hard as she could try, and she had been trying very hard, not to think about it, Jessica knew in the subterranean chambers of her cold, cold heart that Dancer Dawkins and catastrophe were on their way.

SECOND-HAND ROSE

Fatin Satin Aspen twirled his mustache. His gray beard flowed in an avalanche of waves down his immense chest and ended just below his rib cage. Sitting in the rose garden was one of his favorite pastimes. Cushions of daffodils bloomed along the border. Tulips rubbed elbows with iris stalks while freesias sprayed the air with lavender and light fragrance. Fatin Satin Aspen looked fondly at his bed of roses. The sterling silver hybrids were maturing exquisitely. After lying and cheating, he liked those second best.

REVELATION

Fatin Satin Aspen was born Morris Minnow. His mother, Mary, named him after her favorite TV personality, Morris the Cat. While Morris was growing up he discovered that a good lie could reap certain benefits.

"Morris, have you seen my purse?"

"No, Mother."

"Well, that's funny. I could have sworn I put it on the night-stand."

"Oh, here it is, Mother."

"Such a good boy.... Oh dear, I thought I had several quar-ters for the collection plate, but I must have been mistaken."

On Sundays Morris would help his mother by carrying bags of yarn and dozens of darning needles to the neighborhood church hall. There, sitting in a large circle, awaiting their ar-rival, would be twenty to thirty women. While a Brandenburg concerto blared in the background, Mary and the women would sit and knit, and dunk an occasional donut. Some days, Mary would read the latest letter from Violia Vincente, their fearless leader. Sometimes, Violia included pictures of the pagan babies their knitting helped to clothe. "Remember, sisters, how much more fortunate we Americans are." All of Violia's messages ended this way.

Mary Minnow clucked happily to herself; she liked nothing better than the clicking of darning needles. Every summer she and Morris took trips abroad. One year it was Eastern Europe. Another year it was Central America. By the time he was sixteen Morris was a well-traveled boy.

When Mary died she left everything to Morris.

The house.

"Big deal," said Morris.

Bank accounts.

"Not bad," he muttered.

California vineyards.

"Interesting," he thought.

A dresser full of correspondence addressed to Mary Minnow, from Violia Vincente alias Mary Minnow.

"Violia Vincente alias Mary Minnow? Alleluia," screamed Morris, "I am rich, rich, rich."

LIKE MOTHER, LIKE SON

Morris Minnow could not garner the respect that was due the titular head of Violia Vincente without changing his name. He chose Fatin Satin Aspen because of the exotic nature of the rhyming scheme. His first act, as supreme head, was to move the entire outfit to California. Once there, he inquired after his vineyards, and purchased Mount Ascension, a Catholic women's college gone kaput, primarily for the rose gardens and large parking lots. Within three years the business doubled. The complete line now included sweaters, mufflers, and watchcaps. Fatin Satin Aspen cultivated his bed of roses; he shrewdly tacked "Venerable Brigade" on for class. Recruits poured in. Wool garments flowed out, to faraway ports like Uruguay, Hong Kong, or the Andes. There the shipment would be met, labeled, and rerouted back to Canada and the US. By the time he was thirty, Fatin Satin Aspen was a millionaire twice over and set his sights on a more lucrative project. Greed begat greed. Mary Minnow would have been proud.

POOL

Dancer and the Kid slept like two barnacles clinging to the side of a fishing pier. The bed in Ta Jan's extra room was piled high with quilts and soft down comforters. The Kid stripped down to a t-shirt and climbed into the bed. Dancer turned the light off and unbuttoned her shirt.

"Hey, Kid, it's five o'clock and the sun's coming up."

The Kid popped open an eye and watched Dancer undress. "Have you ever seen Navratilova hit a forehand?" she asked.

"Uh-uh," said Dancer pulling off her socks. "Am I missing something?"

"Well," replied the Kid, "you have arm muscles just like her."

Dancer removed her glasses and fell in next to the Kid. A longing for Jessica welled up from her thighs. "Here I am in S.F. sharing a bed with a total stranger," she sniffed, "when all I want is to be held by my beloved *hapa-haole*."

A tear welled up in Dancer's eye and rolled down heartache trail. Another tear slid along the trail and nudged the first one into her ear. Plop. Plop. Plop. It was like shooting pool with mercury balls. Dancer turned over on her side and sloshed her face into the pillows.

The Kid reached over from her sleep and pulled the hiccupping Dancer to her. "I was dreaming an immense redwood tree had fallen on top of me," she said softly. "Great clouds of rain appeared on the horizon, and soon I became afraid of drowning."

Dancer's lids fluttered like a pair of drugged sparrows.

The Kid's voice anchored them as daylight charged around the corner.

Three doors down, Killer Shep curled up next to Ta Jan. The house was slowly filling up with dreams.

LONGSHOT

Ta Jan read the morning paper ritualistically. First she made her coffee. Then she unrolled the rubber band from the bulk of the paper and shot it into her neighbor's yard: number 1,182 landed next to number 1,181. Someday a great red and blue rubber tree would sprout as a memorial to all the deceased rubber bands that had been snapped to that colorful spot.

A bronze plaque at the base of the tree would read:

Here lie 3000 rubber
bands who would rather
be in Philadelphia
popping wheelies.

Dancer and the Kid wandered through the long hallway, poking their heads into each room as if they were physicians examining patients, until they discovered Ta Jan in the kitchen. Ta Jan's house, an upper flat one door down from the restaurant, was light and airy with its high ceilings. Two fireplaces helped with the chill on winter days. During the summer Ta Jan threw open the kitchen door, which opened onto a deck. Southern breezes floated through the hallway like a billowing scarf on a lazy day.

Ta Jan looked up from the sports section. She always read the sports section first. The only day she broke tradition was when John Lennon died. "Did you sleep well?" she asked, noting Dancer's red rimmed eyes.

"Yes."

"No."

They both answered simultaneously.

"There's some coffee in the pot and some croissants in the bag," Ta Jan said, studying the racing forms feverishly. "I never put up strangers," she continued, "but last night during your dinner I got a feeling about you two. It's the same feeling I get sometimes when I go to the track and place a bet on a twenty-to-one long shot. Sometimes the horse comes in. And sometimes I lose my shirt. Anyway, you two didn't steal my dog, or last night's receipts, so the horse at least placed."

"Did you ever see the filly Ruffian run?" interrupted Dancer. "Broke my heart when she died," she wistfully said.

"Mine too," echoed Ta Jan, who watched the Kid dip her croissant into coffee.

Dancer pulled out Jessica's last letter and fingered the return address. "Could you tell me how I could get to 8200 Turk Street?"

Ta Jan quickly rose from her chair. "What on earth could you possibly want there?" she asked as she reached for the butter knife and slowly pushed it through the cube.

Killer Shep's head snapped up from the floor. She knew Ta Jan's hand was shaking. She knew Ta Jan knew. And Ta Jan knew the Kid and Dancer knew. "Oh well," thought Killer Shep, "you can't fool all the people all the time."

FORTUNE

"What is it that you know, that we don't know?" asked Dancer curiously, as she watched Ta Jan move around the table.

Ta Jan slid the knife next to her plate and flicked the pat of butter to Killer Shep. The snoozing shepherd snatched it in mid-flight with a spectacular over-the-shoulder catch.

"A long time ago," Ta Jan began, "before the Goose had its beginnings, I worked my way through night school. One evening as I approached the campus a limo shot past me as I walked up *the* hill, which, by the way, was responsible for shaping one eighth of the women's legs in S.F. from flab to fabulous. Seconds later there was a screeching of brakes. I ran up the hill as fast as I could and saw a blind woman crying hysterically over her guide dog. The driver stepped out of the limo, peeled off a twenty-dollar bill and dropped it next to the stricken dog. I've never forgotten the look in the man's eyes, vacant and uncaring, as he left the woman there with her dog. A year later, the campus closed; the man in the limo bought the school, and made it the center for the Venerable Brigade work."

Dancer took off her glasses and groaned. The why-me vultures were beginning to flock. "What's the name of the guy that bought the place?" she said, rubbing her forehead slowly.

"Fatin Satin Aspen."

"You're joking," the Kid replied.

"Unbelievable," said Dancer. "I thought Jessica was kidding when she mentioned his name."

"The truth," answered Ta Jan. "Oh, one more thing, I hear the Brigade is very, very private. They guard their solitude zealously."

"Shit," Dancer exclaimed. "Jessica said security would be tighter than usual because of some Bohemian festival."

"*The* Bohemian Grove festival?" asked Ta Jan.

"I'm not sure." Dancer shrugged, leaning far back in her chair. "Is it important?"

"Well," said Ta Jan slowly, rolling up a shirt sleeve, "what do you know about the Bohemians?"

"The beatniks?" chimed in the Kid.

"*The* Bohemians," repeated Ta Jan. "The exclusive men's club."

"Oh, them!" laughed Dancer. "Aren't they a group of high-powered executives who meet for several weekends?"

"Right," nodded Ta Jan. "The Bohemian Grove, located along the Russian River, is the name of their campsite."

"Got it," said Dancer snapping her fingers together. "This is the famous corporate lost weekend. High jinks, and skits and rituals."

"Must be a West Coast phenomenon," interjected a puzzled Kid, "because I've never heard of the event."

"On paper it looks innocent enough. A group of aging men drinking and cavorting in the redwoods," replied Ta Jan.

"However," she continued.

The Kid closed her eyes. "Why did I ever leave Bangor?" she thought.

"These are some of the wealthiest men in the nation. And supposedly on this weekend many political and economic deals go down."

"A Southern California newspaper labeled this gathering a party given by the corporate ruling class of America. Bechtel, Kerr-McGee. The list goes on and on," added Dancer.

The Kid downed her coffee. "Enough," she growled. "I don't

like the sound of either the Bohemians or this Fatin Satin Aspen," she said glaring at Dancer, who was staring at her empty coffee cup.

"*We*," emphasized Dancer, "are on our way to the Hill." Taking a deep breath she continued, "I met a woman while ago and fell in love. She left me to come here. Maybe it's finished and maybe it's not, and maybe our fortunes have changed. I don't know," she softly said, "but I'm going to find out. I need your help, Kid."

The Kid looked around the table. She was stuck. She had, after all, bashed in Dancer's car door. But all this over another woman?

Ta Jan folded the newspaper. Half of her adult life had been spent falling in and out of love. And now, at forty, she knew the odds on playing the ponies or shooting craps were little better than affairs of the heart. She stood up to clear the table.

Anxiety raced through Dancer's chest. In the kitchen light, the Kid's face looked terrifyingly indifferent. "Well?" Dancer asked.

"Well," the Kid replied, "I gave you my word, but as soon as this is over, I'm moving on."

"Wonderful," exclaimed Dancer, slapping the Kid's shoulder, "what could possibly go wrong?"

MO' ASS

Ta Jan directed Dancer and the Kid to the mountain which was still fondly referred to by ex-alums as "Mo' Ass." Much to their surprise it was only a stone's throw from the Goose.

"I got a bad feeling about this place," muttered the Kid as

she and Dancer drove up the hill, which was littered with signs like "No Gas," "No Food," "No Lodgings," "Stop Trespassing, Blockhead," "This Means You." "Sociable group," Dancer dryly observed as they approached the top of the hill.

The Kid cringed. A skull and crossbones loomed over the entrance way of the main building. "This had better be a piece of cake," she said, turning to Dancer, who was cheerfully taking a hit off her atomizer.

"Pray for me," Dancer replied, "and Kid, don't forget our story."

CHIPS

Dancer leaned on the doorbell. The Kid popped two wads of bubble gum into her mouth. A small mouse had formed under her left eye, and her lip hung over at the edges. She looked like leftovers from the main event, and she felt just as bewildered. The Venerable Brigade business rolled around in her head like rotting apples in a barrel.

"I hear someone coming," Dancer hissed.

The Kid straightened up as a voice boomed out, "If you're Goodwill, United Crusade, the March of Dimes, or the Lung Association, we already gave. If you're none of the above, you have just thirty seconds to state your business before I light a fire under your ass."

Not very promising, Dancer thought as she heard herself say, "My name is Dancer Dawkins. I've traveled five hundred miles to see my sister, Jessica—"

"No visitors," the voice boomed.

"Wait. Wait just a minute," yelled the Kid. "I know you're

still there, I know you are, and I'd—rather, *we*—would like to make a personal contribution to the Brigade. How does half a gram, a C-note, and a side of bacon sound to you?"

"Side of bacon!" said Dancer disbelievingly.

"OK," said the Kid. "Just to show you where my heart is I'll sweeten the deal by tossing in a pound of butterscotch cookies."

"Chocolate chip," said the voice behind the door. "Chocolate chip," nodded the Kid.

"Say 'please,'" said the voice.

Dancer scowled. The Kid grabbed her arm. "Goddammit, Dancer, say 'please.'"

"Please," mumbled Dancer. "What?"

"Please," Dancer yelled.

A great clinking and clanking filled the air as locks tumbled.

With a wild yawning sound, the door swung open; Dancer and the Kid took one last look at the city below, and stepped inside the archway.

SWEET LOU

Marble steps led from the immense archway to a second door which opened into a vast hallway filled with tapestries and medieval fixtures. "This way, you two," motioned their guard, who resembled one of the starting front four of the S.F. Forty-Niners, and whose name happened to be Luciano, "Sweet Lou" to his immediate family, in honor of his insatiable chocolate cravings. "Wait in here," growled Sweet Lou as he deposited Dancer and the Kid in a room with a narrow pink sofa.

"Friendly fellow," Dancer said.

"Louis XV," exclaimed the Kid, pointing to the sofa.

"I wonder who their interior decorator is?" asked Dancer as she ran her hand along the window ledge.

"Probably someone who liked his women in whalebone, and his men in powdered wigs," replied the Kid.

"Hey," a voice boomed at them from the doorway, "who did you two want to see?" Sweet Lou had returned. He was not known for his keen memory.

"Jessica Riggins. Jess rhymes with Tess and Riggins with Higgins. Got that?"

"Jessica Riggins. Jessica Riggins," the voice boomed down the hallway. Sweet Lou rounded the corner and sat in a chair. He filed his nails and polished his boots. He called down to the kitchen for a cup of coffee. Half an hour had elapsed. He had no intention of combing the campus for some pea-brained recruit; besides, he had already forgotten her name.

PROMISES

Dancer's patience was wearing thin. "You'd think these bright people would have an intercom system, or a switchboard," she said to the Kid, who was unwrapping a fresh chew of gum.

The Kid balled up the old wad and stuck it to the underside of the sofa.

Dancer waved her hand at the Kid. "You know, Ta Jan saved our ass with that bribery business. I never would have keyed in on the deprivation factors."

"We aren't out of the woods yet," said the Kid just as Sweet Lou re-entered the room.

"I couldn't find her," he said.

"Couldn't find her?" Dancer asked incredulously. "She's here, isn't she?"

"Well, actually," Sweet Lou lied, "she told me to tell you to come back tomorrow."

"Tomorrow? I'm her flesh and blood, dyed-in-the-wool sister," Dancer sputtered.

"Today is final exam day and she cannot be disturbed." There was a ring of finality in Sweet Lou's voice; the conversation was over.

Dancer's lungs were beginning to make terrible rasping sounds. The Kid nervously sidled up next to Dancer, and took stock of the situation. They both came up to Sweet Lou's belt buckle; he could probably squash them like bugs on a wall and not feel the least bit winded. The Kid nudged Dancer, who was staring through Sweet Lou's solar plexus. "I could probably squash him like a bug on a wall," she thought, "but I won't."

"Dancer, give the man his goodies," the Kid nervously said. Dancer slipped Sweet Lou the half gram and the C-note.

"Where's the cookies and the side of bacon?" Sweet Lou boomed. "You promised me a bag of chocolate chips."

"Tomorrow," pleaded the Kid. "Chocolate chips, and butterscotch, too."

"Fuck the butterscotch," growled Sweet Lou. "There better be chocolate chips tomorrow," he threatened. "Now," he ordered, "cross your hearts."

The Kid and Dancer crossed their hearts.

Sweet Lou propelled them towards the doorway. These two reminded him of a saying that he couldn't fully remember, something to do with snatching babies from a candy store.

ARIES

The Kid's car shot down the hill like a pack of ball bearings on the loose. "We did it," hollered Dancer. "We have that sucker right where we want him. You were so smooth, Kid. You led him just a bit. And *wham*, then you set the hook," chuckled Dancer, shaking her head.

Dancer's praise lit a small bonfire under the Kid's heart. Somewhat shy and reticent as a child, the Kid hid behind her wads of gum and baseball cap, and mumble-mouthed her way through public speaking confrontations. Once she fainted. George and Belle crossed their fingers, hoping that the Kid would outgrow the dilemma. She did not. But, struggling to overcome this fear, the Kid in time uprooted her anxieties and transferred them to what is termed as gephyrophobia, the fear of bridges. What did she have to worry about? There were no bridges in Bangor.

The Kid took a toke of Dancer's joint. "I was afraid back there," she confessed.

"Afraid of the hulk?"

"Afraid of freezing," the Kid replied. "Immobilization of the mouth."

Dancer nodded.

"I hope all this effort is worth it," the Kid continued.

Dancer stared glumly out the window. "What sign are you, Kid?"

"Aries."

"Aries," exclaimed Dancer. "Why did I even bother to ask?" she thought as she sank back into the car seat and closed her eyes. In Dancer's mind, hell would always be a roomful of

Aries without fire exits, and now here she was getting ready to storm the Bastille with a bagful of cookies and an Aries by her side.

LIST

Ta Jan was totaling the weekly receipts when the Kid and Dancer returned. From the glow on Dancer's face, Ta Jan knew the first phase of their plan had been successful. She reached over for a shopping list and handed it to Dancer. "That's exactly what you'll need," she said. "The main ingredient is in a green vial in the medicine cabinet. Follow the recipe precisely, and one more word of caution: no cookies for the dog," admonished Ta Jan, staring squarely through Killer Shep's almond eyes. The Kid reached down and scratched one of Killer's ears. "Here's hoping we don't eat our way back up the hill," Dancer said, waving the list at the Kid.

TA JAN'S CHOCOLATE CHIP COOKIES

Cream one cup of butter with one cup of brown sugar and one cup of white sugar. Beat and add two eggs and one teaspoon of vanilla. Sift and stir in two cups of flour and four tablespoons of flour, one teaspoon of salt, one teaspoon soda.

To all this add one cup of nut meats and one cup of semi-sweet chocolate chips. Stir together. Place a small portion of mixed batter in a separate bowl. Add one teaspoon of the white powder in the green vial. Stir, and bake apart from main batch.

TAPE

Jessica entered Fatin Satin Aspen's inner office. She removed her shoes and stepped on the sparring mat in the middle of the floor. Facing a full-length wall mirror, she bowed to the four elemental spirits and swung gracefully into a tai chi fighting stance. Slowly, she concentrated on each movement; her nerves, on edge all day, rebelled against the strict regimentation of her actions. "Goddammit," she swore, stopping in the middle of a sweeping kick. "I'm all out of sync." Jessica moved off the mat and grabbed her shoes.

Behind the mirror, Fatin Satin Aspen turned off the videotape equipment. He had seen enough. Jessica's emerald eyes made him delirious with excitement. Rubbing his hands together, he tap-danced down the long passageway to his office. "Hot damn! What plans I have for her!"

CURTAINS

Fatin Satin Aspen collected himself and regally walked through the two French doors. Jessica stood in the middle of the room and nodded.

"You are?" he began.

"Jessica Riggins."

"And you wish?"

"I wish to become an emissary," Jessica softly replied.

"The test is a hard one," said Fatin Satin Aspen, seating himself behind his desk. "Are you afraid?"

"Terrified," thought Jessica, ignoring the question.

"The passing rate is not even worth mentioning, but I'll give you a hint. It's more than ten percent and less than twenty-five percent.

"Holy shit," gulped Jessica.

Fatin Satin Aspen placed a tall, slender black vase on his desk. "Roll up your right sleeve," he ordered.

Jessica did as she was told. The vase glistened in the sun like polished ebony. "Lizards or snakes," she thought, "anything but lizards or snakes."

Fatin Satin Aspen smiled cordially. "Come place your hand in this and tell me what you feel."

Jessica plunged her arm into the vase. The top edge nudged her elbow. She moved her hand around and felt hundreds of cylindrical objects. A feeling of nausea swept over Jessica. "This is it, curtains," she thought. "Goodbye, Dancer. Aloha, Mom and Dad."

Fatin Satin Aspen was amused. He saw the fear on Jessica's face; fear of the unknown. Stroking his beard he gazed into Jessica's green eyes and was startled by her cold, trance-like stare.

"Your conclusion?" he hastily asked.

It took all of Jessica's willpower and better judgment to reply, "This is nothing but a jugful of jellybeans."

"And what led you to make that deduction?"

"Halloween night and groping for candy in the dark," replied Jessica, wiping her hand on a towel.

"I see," said Fatin Satin Aspen. "You're very clever."

"So are you," countered Jessica.

"You may go now."

"I passed then, didn't I?" said Jessica, smugly exiting from the room.

"Not without a little help from me," muttered Fatin Satin Aspen, dumping his prize scorpions back into the vase as Jessica closed the door.

GEMS

Ta Jan's flat was bursting with the rich, thick aroma of a pastry shop. The Kid and Dancer baked cookies as fast as they could load trays. Killer Shep lay to the right of the oven, hopelessly drooling before the first batch finished baking. "This is embarrassing," she thought as she licked her lips, hoping the Kid and Dancer had not noticed her infantile behavior.

"Is that pitiful or what?" motioned the Kid to Dancer.

Dancer turned and was greeted by the large, illuminated, woeful eyes of Killer Shep. "How do they know to do that?"

"I've never met a dog that didn't know how to make a spectacle of itself when it was begging. And once they get the act down, well, Katie bar the door."

Dancer munched on a cookie. "Should we?"

The Kid flung a cookie in Killer Shep's direction. The Killer wolfed it down in one gulp, and grinned. A little on the chewy side, but the cookie was as good as Ta Jan's.

"Here comes the last load," said Dancer as she carefully separated the drugged cookies from the rest of the mountainous nest.

"I wonder if they really work?" asked the Kid as she polished off another cookie.

Dancer casually popped her fourth chip down the hatch. "You know," she said, "chocolate chips were never my favorite cookies. I grew up on oatmeal raisin bars and shortbread. But, to get back to your question, why don't you find out?" she gleefully suggested.

The Kid contemplated the smaller plate of cookies and placed her hand on the counter. "To tell you the truth," the Kid said as she fished for a cookie, "I believe Ta Jan. So, instead of eating this little intoxicating gem, I will replace it in its bed of Nembutal nightmares and call it a night."

Dancer sighed. The last thing she needed was a hung-over partner for the long day ahead.

Killer Shep got up from the floor and stretched. The entire evening had netted her one cookie. "One lousy cookie," she muttered, drifting off to the other room. She made a mental note the next time to bring along her accordion and tin cup.

OREOS

Sweet Lou stashed the half gram of cocaine and the hundred dollar bill in the heel of his shoe. He slicked back his hair and glanced at the bags under his eyes: it had been a long night, riddled with bouts of insomnia. Of course, two cups of espresso and six lines of coke had nothing to do with his sleeplessness.

Sweet Lou's mouth watered with anticipation. He had brought half a gallon of milk from the kitchen, a Thermos jug filled with coffee, and a large empty platter to his room. It had been over a year since the last chocolate chip. Sweet Lou had poured himself some coffee. He sincerely hoped the girls didn't double-cross him because he had been known to maim and kill for a mere bag of Oreos.

CRUMBS

Dancer pounded on the door. Sweet Lou was there in a flash, and led them to what Kid had labeled the "pink room." Dancer set a briefcase on the couch and produced four pounds of thick-sliced bacon. Sweet Lou computed this as twenty BLT's.

"Where's the goddamn cookies?" he rasped, looking first at Dancer and then over to the Kid and back at Dancer again.

"We forgot them," replied Dancer somberly.

"You forgot them!" roared Sweet Lou, stamping his feet, clenching his fists and swinging wildly for Dancer, who skirted his mad efforts by circling safely behind the Kid.

The Kid threw up her right hand. "Stop," she yelled. "Can't you take a joke? The cookies, every single last one of them, are safely tucked away in my backpack." And to make her point, the Kid slipped off her pack and dangled it in front of Sweet Lou like grass shrimp on a number-eight hook. "We'll give you a dozen now, to wet your whistle, and the remainder after we see Jessica."

Sweet Lou pondered this offer for thirty seconds. He wanted to show them he wasn't born yesterday so he said, "What makes you two broads think that I can't overpower you and take what I want?"

"You probably could," answered Dancer.

"But the fact is," continued the Kid, "it would be no fun to be left with a bagful of crumbs, because that is exactly what you will be left holding after we both stomp this sack into the ground."

Dancer crossed her fingers.

The Kid felt strangely light-headed. She was on the verge of fainting.

So was Sweet Lou. He could practically taste those chocolate chips. "OK," he said. "OK. OK. We'll do it your way."

Dancer reached into the Kid's backpack and pulled out the doctored cookies. She smilingly passed the bag over to Sweet Lou, who clutched them to his heart. "Who am I supposed to be paging?" he asked.

"Jessica Riggins, remember?" replied an exasperated Dancer.

"Got you," saluted Sweet Lou, feigning sincerity and interest all in the same breath, when in reality his one-dimensional mind couldn't wait to get the fuck out of there. "Uh, see you two in a while," he said as he ducked out the door.

The Kid collapsed weakly on the couch. This girlfriend business was beginning to irk her. She needed a new set of adrenal glands and a stiff drink, and not necessarily in that order.

WATERFALL

By the time Sweet Lou had raced around the corner and sat down in his throne-sized chair, he had eaten four cookies. Within a space of five minutes, one cookie every 37.5 seconds, Sweet Lou had devoured the entire sack. Nembutal coursed through his veins like water rushing towards a fall. Sweet Lou picked the crumbs off his shirt. He felt pleasantly content. Everything was falling into place. Including himself.

DOCKED

Dancer and the Kid sat like two impatient commuters. The Kid sucked on a piece of gum while Dancer fidgeted with her watch. At approximately 1:23, a distinct thud resounded through the hallway.

The Kid and Dancer bolted upright from the couch.

"Could have been an encyclopedia set falling by the wayside."

"Or a sack of potatoes slipping off a cart."

"Or," they both chorused as they rocketed down the hallway, "our chips have finally docked."

STASH

Sweet Lou's body, launching itself from consciousness, landed like a beached whale on the glistening hardwood floor; his last thoughts were, as his vision blurred, "Gee, I need an eye exam."

Dancer rounded the corner first and agilely sidestepped Sweet Lou's body. The Kid, a step and a half behind, could not avoid the stricken mass and flipped head-over-heels into an immense cedar chest.

Dancer scurried from one body to the next. She felt like a paramedic in a disaster movie. "Kid! Hey, Kid," she cried as she cradled the limp figure in her arms. There was no response. "Why does this always happen to me?" she cursed. "Come on, Kid, say something before the roof caves in on us."

The Kid flicked her eyes open and leapt out of Dancer's arms. "Fooled you, didn't I?" she grinned. "Worried, weren't you?" she continued playfully.

Dancer clutched her chest and screamed, "Shit, Kid, that wasn't funny. Listen to me, for chrissake, we have a six-foot brontosaurus lying at our feet and enough potential trouble to fill a milk wagon. Now," she said, quickly looking over her shoulder, "help me find a place to stash the body."

The Kid folded her arms across her chest. Here she was in S.F., sporting a black eye, looking for this stick-in-the-mud's girlfriend, and crashing at a residence presided over by a gambling Korean and a cartoon dog. "I should have never stopped the car," she thought. "I should have just left it in gear and kept on going."

Dancer glanced over at the Kid, who looked awfully strange. "Come and give me a hand," she urged, eying the cedar chest hopefully.

The Kid glared at Dancer. "Why don't you give me a hand for putting up with all of your half-assed antics?"

"Oh god," Dancer swore, "a pissed-off Aries."

"Look at this mess," the Kid angrily exclaimed, pointing at the stricken Luciano. "That's called aggravated assault," she yelled. "This," the Kid tossed her hands into the air, "is called breaking and entering. And this," she cried, "is unmitigated frustration."

Dancer bit her lower lip as the Kid whirled, pulling down a small tapestry.

A low rumbling filled the hallway.

The Kid back-pedaled into Dancer as the walls parted before them like the Red Sea.

MISSION

At the very moment Dancer and the Kid were stashing Sweet Lou in the cedar chest (no mean feat in itself—they folded his body in a semi-fetal position and prayed that consciousness arrived before asphyxiation), Jessica was in retreat high on the roof of the main building, with a pair of binoculars and a bottle of coconut oil.

Choosing a spot from which she could watch the ships sail to and from the bay, she removed her clothing and rubbed her body with oil. She was pleased with the outcome of yesterday's meeting. She had matched wits with the "Reverend Mother" himself on his own turf, and at his own game.

Jessica smiled coyly to herself as she lubricated her calves. She remembered the first time Dancer had come on the top of her thigh; she thought her cries had shattered glass. Capping the bottle, Jessica turned and lay on her stomach.

Four floors beneath her, Dancer and the Kid were examining the switch the Kid had thrown when she yanked the tapestry off the wall.

"It's obviously a family secret," said the Kid, re-hanging the tapestry.

"Some family," sniffed Dancer, waltzing back and forth into the passageway.

"Ready?" asked the Kid.

"With you," replied Dancer as she hit the switch on her side of the tunnel.

The walls slowly closed.

Dancer and the Kid stepped into the passageway: a sense of adventure as well as fear engulfed them. It therefore brought them much comfort and peace of mind, as they entered the unknown, that Dancer's imagination had altered them into paid assassins on a mission of mercy.

CELLAR

Lit up like an airport runway at night, the passageway rambled around several curves, descending sharply towards a long flight of stairs. Dancer, who had led the expedition, dropped back behind the Kid as they cautiously wound their way down the steps.

"Whoever built these stairs knew nothing about angles," muttered the Kid.

Dancer, almost slipping twice, grunted in agreement as the steepness of each step increased in direct proportion to their descent.

"Have you noticed how bright these lights are?" asked the Kid.

"Suits me fine. I hope that when this bottoms out, the way back is not the way we have just come, because I'm not going to like that one bit," grumbled Dancer.

"Neither am I," responded the Kid, pausing to brush the hair from her eyes and peeling herself a fresh wad of gum.

Dancer passed the Kid and waved her around the next corner. "The end of the line," she exclaimed, pointing to an old, weathered door that appeared to be the entranceway to an immense cavern.

"No bats, Dancer. I don't go in if there are any bats," threatened the Kid.

Dancer put her shoulder to the door and pushed. "Gimme

a hand," she gasped. The Kid reluctantly leaned against the door. Grudgingly the door gave way, revealing a wine cellar the size of a football field.

Dancer let out a high-pitched whistle. "Somebody must really like to party, or. . . ."

"Or," interjected the Kid, "this is the best-kept secret since the invention of the spitball."

STUDIO

In his video studio, three stories above the colossal wine cellar, Fatin Satin Aspen replayed the tape he had just finished making. Several years back, an enormous shipment of mufflers had been mistakenly rerouted by an over-zealous lieutenant who misread "Niagara" for "Nigeria," never questioning the fact that wool mufflers in Nigeria were like penguins without an ice floe. Ultimately, the cargo was traced, but not before a hefty under-the-table exchange had transpired between Nigerian customs, who for weeks sat on the shipment waiting to see which honky-ass bozos would file a claim, and a very red-faced Venerable Brigade representative.

Fatin Satin Aspen had been livid. Determined that this mistake never be repeated, he upgraded all his communications to tape recordings. For special high-priority events he retired to his video studio and cranked out his messages on tape.

Fatin Satin Aspen chuckled as he watched himself drone on, cutting back and forth from the tape of Jessica to various wide-angle shots of Napa Valley. His friend Alain was going to heat up like a pistol when he saw the new package he was sending. "Hell," Fatin Satin Aspen snorted, "Alain is going to be punchy when he latches onto those emerald eyes—a classy gesture on my part," Fatin Satin Aspen thought as he rose from his chair, flicking off machinery, turning on lights, and murmuring softly into his beard, "almost as good as gold."

STREAM

Beads of sweat glistened on Jessica's body as she fell asleep under the noonday sun. Her arm jerked aimlessly as a host of dreams streamed towards her sleeping figure much the way the river rushes to meet the sea. Jessica rolled over on her side. She was dreaming of a large steamer captained by a man who wore a Kabuki mask. Clouds of smoke billowed off the horizon as the ship spilled onto a coral reef. Overhead, a host of aircraft dropped from the sky, strafing the ocean with yellow dust. Jessica lurched from sleep. Sitting upright, she buried her face in a towel. A light breeze drifted over the rooftop as Jessica groped for her watch: she had been napping for twenty minutes.

BEER

The Kid wandered between rows and rows of bottles, stacked like fallen trees in a petrified forest; examining different labels she discovered the cumbersome immobility of such words as Cabernet Sauvignon, Johannesburg Riesling, and Pinot Chardonnay. She preferred the lilting quality of Zinfandel and Gamay Beaujolais, but next to baseball and a good Cubano, there was nothing like a cold bottle of beer. Wine was for pansies who sat around all day nibbling Brie and pâté, and the California Kid was no pansy.

PANSY

Dancer walked through the aisles as if she were pushing a shopping cart. Could it be that her karma had finally delivered her into paradise? Dancer took a deep breath and purred as her fingers lightly traced the origin of certain bottles. She estimated the value of the entire wine cellar to be a conservative half million. Dancer closed her eyes and leaned against an oak cask. She was on the verge of having an orgasmic seizure when the Kid's voice short-circuited her mind.

"What's all this shit?" she heard the Kid boom.

ASH

Ta Jan was flipping through the mail addressed to the Golden Goose when a pale blue envelope embellished with silver border caught her eye. Leaning over, she glided the envelope past Killer Shep's nose.

Killer Shep raised her upper lip and scowled. She was in a testy mood: two alley cats had wreaked havoc with her sleep. This morning, bags swelling under her eyes like pastry puffs, she had retreated to the comfort and security of Ta Jan's kitchen, never to be disturbed again, she hoped, until the envelope descended on her like a handful of volcanic ash. Squinting at Ta Jan she said, "I hate to be the bearer of bad tidings, but that letter smells like trouble."

Ta Jan took a sip of her coffee and slit the envelope open.

"Listen to this," Ta Jan said to the sleeping dog.

"I'm sleeping," said the dog.

"Dear Ta Jan," began the letter. "Your culinary expertise has been brought to my attention. If you are interested in catering a dinner party for 150 people, please call 678-6774. Sincerely, Fatin Satin Aspen. PS: Your fee is highly negotiable."

"You woke me for that?" exclaimed Killer Shep. "Of course we're not going to accept," she continued. "That cat"—a derogatory dig at Fatin Satin Aspen—"is already one for one in the canine department: I don't intend to become another statistic."

Ta Jan drummed her fingers on the countertop, and picked up the phone. Punching in the numbers, she turned her back on Killer Shep. "Perhaps," she mused, "there was some truth behind the old saying to let sleeping dogs lie."

HAMMER

Fatin Satin Aspen let his private phone ring three times before he answered it.

"Hello," he purred.

"Hello," replied the voice on the other end. "I'm calling in regard to a letter I received concerning my culinary talents."

Fatin Satin Aspen's ears perked up.

So did Killer Shep's.

"Is this the esteemed owner of the Golden Goose?" Fatin Satin Aspen asked rather cagily.

"Yes, it is," replied an unimpressed Ta Jan.

"Wonderful," cooed Fatin Satin Aspen.

"I presume I am speaking with Fatin Satin Aspen," said Ta Jan.

"The honorable Fatin Satin Aspen."

Ta Jan looked dryly at the receiver. "Your self-esteem is limitless."

Fatin Satin Aspen let out a nervous chuckle.

"How did you happen to choose the Golden Goose?" asked Ta Jan curiously.

"Your reputation as a gourmet cook precedes you," answered Fatin Satin Aspen. "In culinary circles, they speak your name with reverence."

"Flattery will get you nowhere," thought Ta Jan, as she began, "My fee. . . ."

"Your fee," interrupted Fatin Satin Aspen, "should be discussed over lunch."

"That is highly presumptuous of you," snapped Ta Jan. "I never discuss business over meals."

"A little sushi," purred Fatin Satin Aspen. "A taste of sashimi. And some hot saki."

"I never mix business with pleasure," reiterated Ta Jan coldly. "And furthermore," she said, "I'm Korean, not Japanese."

"What's the goddamn difference?" thought Fatin Satin Aspen. "Look," he finally said.

"No, you look. The difference is in the eye of the beholder."

Fatin Satin Aspen was peeing in his pants.

Ta Jan smothered a laugh and blew Killer Shep a kiss.

"Now," she said, "my fee will be $150 for the consultation, and $3500 if I accept the job."

Ta Jan's words hit Fatin Satin Aspen like a sledgehammer. Used to getting something for nothing, Fatin Satin Aspen was speechless. He cleared his throat, as if to reassure himself that he had not been struck dumb.

"Very well," he whispered.

"Good," said Ta Jan. "Now that everything is in order: lunch, at your place, one o'clock tomorrow," she said, hanging up.

Fatin Satin Aspen held the receiver in his hand for several seconds before slamming it to the floor. He knew he had been skewered and roasted like a pig on a spit.

BREW

Dancer peered over the Kid's shoulder. Behind a row of oak casks tucked way into a dark corner were five stainless-steel containers. Dancer put her hands on her hips. Sometimes the Kid could be really dense. "Those are probably aging vats for a pressing of Chardonnay," she smugly said.

The Kid glared at Dancer. What a bonehead. "You don't think I called you over here for a crash course in wine-making? Take a closer look."

Dancer edged forward and noticed iridescent decals on the bottom left corner of each vat. "Skull and crossbones," she murmured. "But why would anyone put that on a wine cask?"

"And look at this," the Kid said, walking behind the row of metal drums. "The bottom of each container has been marked with a slash of orange paint."

"Definitely a strange brew," remarked a puzzled Dancer.

"Too strange. I don't know jack about wine," said the Kid, "but five will get you ten there's no grapes in that pressing."

"Oh, come on, Kid, that's probably just someone's private reserve of—"

"Of rotgut," interjected the Kid.

"Listen, pal, you may be the victim of an overly active mind," mused Dancer, who knew what she was talking about since she owned one of the world's most overactive minds.

"You don't happen to have a can opener on you?" asked the Kid.

"For one of those?" exclaimed Dancer, pointing to the line of steel vats.

"For this," said the Kid, pulling a tin of sardines from her backpack.

"Wait a minute," motioned Dancer. "Shh. I thought I heard a noise."

A low droning filled the air.

"It sounds like an elevator lift," said the Kid.

"It is an elevator lift," agreed Dancer. "And it's heading this way."

The Kid and Dancer looked wildly around. "Well, the way I see it," said the Kid, "we can stand here and get caught with our pants down, or we can take our chances through that door over there."

Dancer turned in the Kid's direction. "Let's do it," she said, bolting across the room in true gridiron fashion.

The elevator slowly ground to a halt. Fatin Satin Aspen stepped into his wine cellar just as the Kid and Dancer disappeared from view.

HYBRIDS

Jessica focused the binoculars on a large freighter steaming into port. From her vantage point on the roof, she had an unobstructed view of the bay, the hills beyond it, and the city below. Sometimes, on foggy days, a layer of clouds perched itself, rolling over rooftops, hovering like so many silver-winged things, extinguishing bay and topography in one swoop. When Jessica first saw this, the sight took her breath away.

Drifting off the bay, Jessica scanned the grounds beneath her. The library building loomed to the right, and beyond it the rose garden. Jessica slowly swung the glasses across the garden. It was impeccable: even the Red Queen would be hard pressed to find fault. Pausing to admire the landscaping, Jessica retrained the binoculars on the hedges hugging the library wall. Something was stirring behind them. Quickly refocusing, she followed the train of movement until it stopped at the edge of the rose garden.

Two faces bloomed forth from the vegetation like hybrids.

"Oh god," cried Jessica, "it's Dancer."

CAKE

When the Kid and Dancer fled the wine cellar they found themselves within another tunnel. Ever grateful for the high-intensity voltage that illuminated their way, they proceeded cautiously along a circuitous route which eventually fragmented into two paths. To their left, the tunnel dead-ended with a door. To their right, the tunnel appeared to continue.

"I opt for the door," said Dancer, wiping off her glasses. "How about you?"

"It's definitely the door," agreed the Kid. "I don't care what's behind it as long as it's not another tunnel."

"Shall we?"

"After you," said the Kid.

Dancer put her hand on the doorknob. "This reminds me of a dream I once had where I opened a door, only to find another door, and opening that door, I found yet another."

"Will you open the goddam door?"

Dancer slowly opened the door. Fresh air and dappled sunlight engulfed them. They stood quietly for several seconds, letting the wind pass over them in waves.

"It seems," said Dancer, peering around, "that we're sandwiched between a row of hedges and a building wall."

"A piece of cake," said the rejuvenated Kid, stepping out of the tunnel and into the daylight.

RE-WRITE

Jessica set a modern-day record for dressing. She tossed on her clothes in a wave of reckless abandon. The shoelaces she tied in double knots; she didn't want to risk breaking her neck before she broke someone else's. In a blur of frenzy, Jessica took the staircase. Bounding through the hallway onto the campus, Jessica gritted her teeth. The thought of Dancer Dawkins foraging through Brigade property spurred her to new heights of aerobic endurance. Last week, a time of 4:18.08 was set for the women's mile. Jessica smiled grimly to herself. After today, they may have to re-write the record books.

PHOTO

Dancer and the Kid popped out of the hedges like slices of bread from a toaster. The Kid brushed herself off. Her hair was covered with bits of twig and leaf and her mouth felt like a bed of crackers. Breaking open a fresh wad of gum the Kid turned and gazed at the route they had traveled. The hedges, like a string of boxcars, sat back against a towering, whitewashed building. Across the way, a low stucco wall ringed the perimeter of the campus.

"Jesus Christ, what a view," said Dancer, motioning the Kid towards her. "I forgot how elevated we were."

"That's not the only thing you forgot," said a voice behind them. "Did you come here to pick the roses, or to admire the view?"

Dancer spun around. Her heart was thudding against her shirt. "Jessica," she exclaimed.

The Kid, pivoting into the greenest eyes that had ever splashed across her frame, nearly swallowed her gum. "Jessica," she repeated foolishly, her heart booming somewhere within her chest.

"Is there an echo here, or am I just hearing things?" said Jessica, leaning forward and kissing Dancer.

The Kid looked down at her boots.

Jessica, embracing Dancer, looked over at the Kid.

That picture was worth a thousand words.

DANCE

Eternity is the desert flower before the bloom.

The Kid stood for an eternity, slowly counting to ten. Her mind had derailed and lay in an excitable heap at Jessica's feet. Turning away from Dancer and Jessica, the Kid contemplated the source of her feelings. She was alone, in a strange city, wandering hand in hand with an asthmatic lunatic in search of her girlfriend. Better it had been the Holy Grail. Because it looked like trouble.

Dancer's voice shook the peaches from the Kid's tree. "Kid, I'd like you to meet the pride of the Hawaiian Islands, Jessica Nahale Riggins."

Jessica extended her hand.

The key turned in the lock.

And all the clocks stopped.

The Kid clasped Jessica's hand and heard herself say, "mumblemumblemumble." What she really wanted to say was: "Hi, my name is the California Kid. Do you want to dance?"

COACH

Fatin Satin Aspen walked paternally through his wine cellar. He fondled a Chardonnay here and a Sauvignon there. Cautiously weaving his way among the bottles, he drifted towards the five steel containers which had puzzled Dancer and the Kid. Patting each affectionately, the way a coach pats the ass of a prize player, Fatin Satin Aspen gloated over his clever scheme, which would soon give him undisputed control of the entire California wine industry. Money bought power. And power shaped the future. Isn't that, after all, what life as a Boho was all about?

POWDER KEG

Jessica's emerald eyes met the pale blue irises of the Kid's the way a field of corn hugs the sky in the early summer light.

Dancer was no dummy. She saw the charged exchange and bit her lower lip. Ignoring the pageantry unfolding before her she nervously swiveled her head and said, "I don't think we should be standing around here like this. We're in full view of those windows."

The Kid snapped back to life and heard Jessica say, "The California Kid? What part of California?"

"Maine. Bangor, Maine," answered the Kid.

"Makes perfect sense," laughed Jessica, her eyes sparkling like party glitter in a pool of sun.

"Did you hear what I said?" groused Dancer, rapidly approaching asthmatic countdown.

"Of course we did, dear," smiled Jessica diplomatically, while wishing she could land a right cross on Dancer's chin for this sudden invasion of privacy.

Dancer grinned back at her through clenched teeth. She felt like a powder keg embedded in a shifting mountainside.

GINGER

Ta Jan sat at the kitchen counter chewing on her conversation with Fatin Satin Aspen. She brewed herself some coffee and formulated a plan with a built-in escape clause. Reaching into a brown clay pot she unearthed a handful of gingersnaps. Ginger cleansed the palate and stimulated the mind. "We must be careful," she said to a snoozing Killer Shep. "This is a domineering man who has few apparent weaknesses. Fortunately," she said, assembling several knives before her, "we know what one of them is. And," she continued, addressing the sleeping dog while she drew the blades across a whetstone, "we are going to use that to our full advantage."

YANKEE STADIUM

Jessica herded Dancer and the Kid down a short flight of stairs into the library building. "We can't just wander the hallways like this," she said, opening the door to a small lecture room and leading them into it. "You two don't look like you belong here, and if someone notices, Jesus, I could lose my emissary status."

"Let's talk about that," growled Dancer, leaning against the lectern.

"About what?" asked the irked Kid, who realized she was caught in a family squabble.

"Emissary. That word emissary," spat Dancer, who circled Jessica like a boxer looking for an inside opening.

Jessica stood unflinchingly in the middle of the room and stared coldly at Dancer. "If you don't mind," she began, "I don't intend to publicly air our dirty laundry. But," she continued, her voice angrily rising, "may I remind you that you are fucking trespassing on my private property."

The Kid cleared her throat. "Too bad I'm not a ring on the finger of Jessica's hand," she nervously thought. "I know," she said aloud, "that you two have a lot to discuss. I also know the perfect place you can have this discussion." Her voice slowly dropped. "The wine cellar."

Dancer looked blankly at the Kid. "The wine cellar?"

"The wine cellar. What wine cellar?" asked Jessica.

"*The* wine cellar," repeated the Kid.

"You mean," said Dancer, turning to Jessica, "that you don't know there's a wine cellar that looks like—"

"Yankee Stadium," cut in the Kid.

"Well," said Dancer smugly, "come follow me."

WHISTLE

The Kid waved Dancer aside and led the way back to the hidden door; she felt like she was riding point on a cattle drive.

All she wanted was to make her delivery and head out for the nearest watering hole. The debt she owed to Dancer was paid, and as titillating as their encounter was, the Kid knew that an involvement with Jessica would be like free-falling without a parachute.

"Here we are," said Dancer, as the Kid opened the door to the tunnel.

"Incredible," gasped Jessica, as she looked around in disbelief. "It's mind-boggling to realize that someone went to all this trouble to excavate these passages. Where does that lead?" she asked, motioning to the right.

"We don't know," replied the Kid. "When we reached this point, we opted for the door."

"And the wine cellar?"

"That's at the bottom of this tunnel," answered Dancer.

"Look, if you two don't mind," said the Kid, "I'm going to explore this other passageway; I need a breather, and you two need to take care of business. Meet you in the wine cellar in an hour."

"Wait a minute, Kid," said Dancer. "I don't know how safe it is for you to wander around. Perhaps we should all stick together and not push our luck."

The Kid mulled over Dancer's reasoning. She was absolutely right. There was strength in numbers. There was only one small problem: The Kid wanted to be alone.

Jessica crossed her legs and sat down against the tunnel wall. "I have an idea," she said. "Dancer, we don't have to trudge all the way to the wine cellar: we can stay here and talk. Kid, you can go off and explore, and if you need us, just whistle."

Dancer gazed admiringly at Jessica. What a bright and clever girl she was.

The Kid nodded appreciatively at Jessica. "By the way," she said, turning to go, "I don't know how to whistle."

PLUNK

Jessica reached up and pulled Dancer down beside her. She was cross and irritated with Dancer's breach of security. Why couldn't she have gone through the proper channels? If she had, they wouldn't be huddled together like sewer rats in the bowels of the old school. Jessica ran her fingers through her hair. Of course, she reasoned, these were presumptions one could make of a normal, functioning human being. Remembering that Dancer's mind was stuck somewhere between Cuisinart and Waring blender, Jessica prepared herself for the unexpected.

Dancer cupped both of Jessica's hands to her lips and kissed her fingertips. "I love these hands," she softly said. "And I've missed you. God, how I've missed you. I could whisper sweet nothings in your ear all day, and forgive your recent mistakes."

"Just like that," broke in Jessica.

"Just like that," assured Dancer, nibbling on her ear.

"How," asked Jessica, whose concentration was careening off the tunnel walls, "did you manage to get in?"

"We drugged the big ape at the door," said Dancer, slowly unbuttoning the top of Jessica's robe.

"You drugged Sweet Lou?"

"We wasted him," nodded Dancer emphatically.

"You really drugged Sweet Lou?" repeated Jessica incredulously. "Dancer, do you know what you've done?"

"Uh-uh," murmured Dancer. "But I know what I'm about to do."

Jessica closed her eyes and felt her mind dribble down the drain. She also heard the muscles in her thighs go plunk, plunk, plunk, like a guitar being tuned and prepared to play.

Jessica slid Dancer's Levi's off and took a stroll down memory lane. "Before . . . before we go any further," panted Jessica, "let me get this straight. Sweet Lou is stashed somewhere like a mop in a broom closet."

"Check."

"Unconscious but not dead?"

"Check again."

"Uh, god," moaned Jessica, who, unlike Sweet Lou, was about to experience heaven on earth, "I hope we don't regret this."

JUNGLE

The Kid followed the tunnel as it wound sharply uphill. She was grateful for Jessica's insight and suggestion. Being alone and in a strange place was not a comforting thought, but being alone and away from Dancer was like a paid holiday.

The Kid paused to catch her breath. She was beginning to feel a little claustrophobic. A low hum from the lighting system circulated through the upper level, and in certain areas the ventilation had noticeably tailed off. Hot and sweaty, the Kid pushed on; she was imagining herself a Sherpa in the wilds of the Himalayas, when the appearance of a blue door with an elaborate brass motif depicting a levitating donut over a cup of coffee startled her from her daydreams.

The Kid stifled a laugh and ran her hand over the donut, which was flanked by a pair of darning needles. She wondered what manner of mind would elevate the humble cake donut to celestial status.

Placing her ear over the darning needles, the Kid took a long listen, and cautiously opened the door. Light poured from the tunnel into the darkened room, honeycombing it with shadows. The Kid groped along the wall and flicked a light switch. Pieces of video equipment and immense shipping cartons lay scattered before her. Walking slowly through a jungle of cords and camera lights the Kid paused before a video machine. The cassette that was nestled inside the videotape recorder bore Jessica's name. The Kid's eyes lit up; she carefully scrutinized the equipment. The words *eject, play, fast forward*, and *rewind* assaulted her memory. Pushing the power button and hitting the *play* slot set the tape in motion without any audio or video effects. The Kid stood there puzzled. Frustrated after trying several different combinations, the Kid flicked on the TV set. The screen glowed silently. Punching the *play* button in despair, the Kid began rifling through sheets of paper when the TV screen jumped to life. Images of Jessica darted across the tube. "Hello Alain," said a large, portly man. The Kid sat down in a metal chair. Peeling herself a fresh chew did not prepare her for what followed.

SUBWAY

Jessica stroked Dancer's hair and kissed the bridge of her nose. Skipping deliriously across a cheekbone, Jessica nestled her tongue in the pocket of Dancer's mouth. "Look at us," she said. "I love this body of yours."

Dancer took Jessica's hand and guided it over her breasts. "Feel how soft my nipples have gotten," she quietly urged.

"Is this another invitation?" Jessica coyly asked, swinging her lips down Dancer's collarbone and lightly brushing both of her breasts.

"I think I hear my mother calling," said Dancer.

"You what?" laughed Jessica, hovering over Dancer like an angel poised above a bouquet of nectar.

"Well," said Dancer, "I think it's safe to assume that our hour is almost up."

Jessica playfully braided Dancer's pubic hair.

"One of us has to take the bull by the horns," said Dancer, tumbling Jessica over on her back. "We can't pretend to be screwing in the New York subway system all day. Besides, the Kid's due back."

"Well, let's ask her to join: we could have a glorious ménage," exclaimed Jessica, stepping into her robe.

Dancer turned her back on Jessica and ignored the last remark. A smattering of lines had fallen across her forehead; anxiety replaced pleasure, trauma uprooted tranquility. Buttoning her shirt, she said firmly to Jessica, "We have got to talk. Before I go crazy."

"Too late for that," Jessica thought as Dancer took her hand and led them both in the direction the Kid had taken. "We might as well meet the Kid halfway," Dancer glumly said.

"Oh, babe, of course we'll talk," Jessica soothed in a voice reserved for mad dogs and lovers. "And hopefully before Sweet Lou comes to," she muttered.

PEARLS

The Kid sat in stunned silence as the tape rolled to a finish. She pressed the *rewind* button, and checked her pulse. "Still ticking," she raved feverishly as she shut down the system and bolted for the door. Retracing her steps, the Kid broke into a fast sprint. Her mind clicked on and off like a strobe light. "I need a drink. I need a drink," she heard it repeat as she hot-footed down the tunnel path, twisting around turns like Janet Gutherie breaking for the straightaway and launching herself past a frightened Dancer and Jessica, who had flattened themselves against a tunnel wall in anticipation of whoever or whatever was coming their way.

"Jesus Christ, Kid, thank god it's you," exclaimed a relieved Dancer, as the Kid ground to a sudden halt.

Leaning over and clutching her knees, the Kid inhaled slowly several times. Her face was blotched with color as her lungs filled with air. "This guy, Fatin Satin Aspen," she gasped, "is a fucking asshole. He's got plans to destroy the entire Napa Valley. And that's not all—"

"Wait a minute," seethed Jessica.

"No, you wait a minute," yelled the Kid. "As for you, he's got special plans for you. He's planning to ship you off to a pal of his in France, so you can lie around and give him head all day. And there's more," the Kid continued, "but I want you to see for yourself."

Dancer went over and patted the Kid's shoulder. "Take it

easy, Kid. Take it easy," she calmly said. "Come on. Breathe deep. Breathe deep."

The Kid looked over at Jessica, who was as pale as a string of pearls under glass. "Are you all right?" she asked.

"Show me," Jessica gritted.

The Kid turned around and led them to the viewing room.

DALLAS COWBOYS

92   Sweet Lou dreamed that he was running along the beach. As hard as he tried he could not get near the water. Sweat dribbled down Sweet Lou's face as the heat hung over his head like a bunch of rotting bananas. With one final effort Sweet Lou lunged forward, his legs pumping wildly for the surf.

Fatin Satin Aspen, on his way to the infirmary to collect a supply of "whites," was approximately three feet from his beloved mother Mary's antique cedar chest when it exploded like a chocolate-covered egg. Out popped Sweet Lou. His first word was "Duhhh" as he clutched his Nembutal-soaked noggin. His next words were "I'm going to kill those bitches."

Fatin Satin Aspen, who almost equaled Sweet Lou in stature, led the drugged chipaholic to a chair. He peered into his eyes and pinched the blood back into his cheeks. Tilting Sweet Lou's head against the edge of the chair, Fatin Satin Aspen wet down a scarf and applied it to the stricken guard's forehead.

Sweet Lou opened his eyes and shut them rapidly. "Shit," he thought, "it's the boss." His mind turned like a feeble butter churn in search of a good excuse.

Fatin Satin Aspen took the open palm of his right hand and slapped Sweet Lou's face briskly. "Now that we know you're awake"—he used the royal "we" occasionally—"we would like to be filled in as to what took place here. You, my dear boy, look as if you were hit by a bus."

Sweet Lou tried to think fast. "Well," he began weakly, "I was attacked by a couple of leftovers from the Dallas Cowboys training camp. They pushed their way in at the front door and kept on going. I swear, Boss, I didn't have a chance. They would have mugged your own mother."

"God rest her soul," said Fatin Satin Aspen, stroking his beard. He added rather thoughtfully, "You mentioned something about those 'bitches.'"

The blood rushed to Sweet Lou's face. "I must have been delirious," he lied.

Fatin Satin Aspen stared into space. What was going on here? Perhaps this was a joke. One of his fellow Bohos testing security? Sending up some muscle to run amok in the Rose Garden? What a laugh. Besides, all the valuables were in the wine cellar, and you had to be part gopher in order to find that.

"Excuse me, Boss," Sweet Lou said politely, not wishing to be a wrench in the cogs of Fatin Satin Aspen's glowing mind, "but should I straighten this tapestry?" He pointed brightly to a slightly faded fifteenth-century hunting scene.

Fatin Satin Aspen turned towards Sweet Lou. The blood drained from his face and his pulse skyrocketed. "We had better get our asses into gear," he roared. "You," pointing to Sweet Lou, "come with me."

2,4,5-T

The Kid flicked off the lights and popped in the cassette. Jessica leaned forward, neck muscles tightening, as she stalked herself on tape. "This was filmed yesterday," she said as she watched herself moving in and out of different *katas*. "Which means," she added, "that the full-length mirror in Fatin Satin Aspen's office is a two-way fixture."

"Son of a bitch," snapped Dancer, who moved in closer towards Jessica.

The Kid, who sat behind both of them on a long table, packed her cheek with gum as footage of the Napa Valley gave way to Fatin Satin Aspen's immense frame.

Dancer recoiled at the sight of him. Secretly she was pleased at the turn of events. Jessica was a very headstrong woman, and Dancer had not relished the idea of trying to convince her to take a second look at the entire Brigade concept.

Jessica's shoulders curled into the crook of Dancer's arm. She braced herself for the worst.

Dancer studied Fatin Satin Aspen intently. "These cult leader types always seem to have beards," she whispered to Jessica.

"Hello Alain, how are things in Aix?" greeted Fatin Satin Aspen. "Well, what do you think of your new emissary? Pretty young thing, isn't she, and those eyes, such marvelous jewels," he crooned. "Rather exquisite against that supple body, don't you think? Consider her a gift, a pre-2,4,5-T victory celebration." Here Fatin Satin Aspen's face broke into a toothless smile. "As you can see from the film, the target area is not very large at all. However, my pilot has informed me that it will take several passes to complete the job. Then we wait for the foliage to drop. And when it does, my friend, you and I will be very wealthy men."

An ocean of silence filled the room, as the Kid stopped the tape and flicked on the lights. Stepping over cords and wandering through a maze of shipping crates she searched the back area for another chair.

Jessica felt a chill run through her body. Her palms were wet, and her skin clammy. In a month she would have been farmed out like a piece of exported Brigade merchandise, never to be heard from again. Jessica fought back a wave of nausea. Turning to Dancer, her eyes narrowing in the light, she asked, "Is 2,4,5-T what I think it is?"

Dancer took off her glasses and rubbed her temples. The situation was much worse than she imagined. "I think," she said, "that 2,4,5-T is some kind of herbicide. Am I right, Kid?"

Before the Kid could say anything, the door burst open and there under the archway, holding a semi-automatic weapon, stood Sweet Lou, and behind him, Fatin Satin Aspen.

POX

As Sweet Lou crossed the threshold of the room, the Kid, hidden by several large shipping crates, hit the viewing room floor. Scrambling on all fours to keep from being discovered, the Kid worked her way among the crates until she was enclosed on all sides by packing apparatus.

"Well, well," the Kid heard Fatin Satin Aspen say, "what do we have here?"

Jessica, restrained by the nickel-plated barrel of Sweet Lou's gun, glared at Fatin Satin Aspen. Her first impulse was to bury him under a flurry of blows.

Dancer, wishing she had never left the comforts of her Southern California home, cringed when she saw Sweet Lou's six-foot-four bulk advancing towards her.

Sweet Lou, registering relief and ecstasy upon spying Dancer, shouted, "It's them, Boss, it's them," inadvertently blowing the whistle on his alibi.

Fatin Satin Aspen surveyed the room. What was this imbecile shouting about? There were only four people present, and two of them were girls. Fatin Satin Aspen stared intently at Sweet Lou as the chips fell into place. "Is this the linebacker that mugged you at the front door? Well, is it?" he cried, grabbing Dancer by the shoulder and shoving her against the wall.

Sweet Lou looked like the cat who had swallowed the canary. "There were two of them," he sheepishly confessed.

"Two of them," blinked Fatin Satin Aspen. "Well, where's the other one?" he roared.

Dancer looked up and caught Jessica's eye. The Kid was nowhere in sight.

Fatin Satin Aspen turned his back on Dancer and stepped behind a frightened Jessica. Yanking her head back, he hissed, "I see we've been watching videotapes. Anything interesting?" He reached under Jessica's robe and tossed her knife to the floor.

"You fucking pig," swore Jessica.

Fatin Satin Aspen smiled to himself. "Too bad for Alain," he thought as he struck Jessica across the mouth.

Dancer surged forward and was shoved back into the wall by Sweet Lou.

"I'm a civilized man, Jessica," Fatin Satin Aspen snapped, "and I don't like to expend my energy violently, but where is your other friend?" he asked as he struck her again.

Dancer's system heaved towards overload. Her lungs sounded like drowning organ pipes. Slipping under Sweet Lou's arm, she rushed Fatin Satin Aspen, knocking him to the ground with a flying leap to the kidneys.

"There isn't any other person, you pig," she yelled, as Sweet Lou leveled her with a blow to the side of the head.

Fatin Satin Aspen brushed himself off. "Enough of this bullshit," he thought. "Who's in charge here anyway?" Turning to Sweet Lou, he said, "I want you to take these two and let them cool their heels in the deep freeze while I think of some clever plan to rid us of this pox."

Sweet Lou nodded. His brain stumbled over the word "pox." The boss must have meant foxes.

"Then," continued Fatin Satin Aspen, "I want you to search the entire campus beginning with the wine cellar. Go over everything with a fine-toothed comb. *Comprende*?"

"Yeah, Boss, comb."

"Brother," muttered Fatin Satin Aspen, "I need a 'lude. Now get these two out of my sight."

Sweet Lou slung Dancer over his shoulder and left the room with Jessica in tow.

Fatin Satin Aspen placed his hands on his hips. What a fiasco. A total fucking breakdown of security on the eve of perhaps the greatest event of his life. Flicking off the lights and closing the door, he paused before the brass motif. "Mom," he said, patting the donut, "you were right. Good help is hard to find."

The Kid, numb and stricken with fear, crawled out of her hiding place and retched once before passing out.

FREEZE-DRIED

Sweet Lou deposited Dancer and Jessica in an abandoned meat locker behind the school cafeteria. Several large hooks dangled from the ceiling, and a foul, musty odor hung in the air.

Pushing Jessica into the middle of the room, Sweet Lou dropped Dancer in a heap on the sawdust-covered floor. "You're lucky," he said, "that the reason we don't use this freezer anymore is because the refrigeration gave out months ago. Otherwise, you two would be nothing but freeze-dried chips in the morning."

Sweet Lou stopped and wiped the sweat from his forehead. He was ticked at himself for being such an asshole. He felt cheated and deceived. Worse still, he felt set up and used.

Turning to Jessica and running the nose of the gun under her chin, he said, "When that bitch comes to, you tell her Sweet Lou owes her. You also tell her that when I find her partner, I'm going to squash her like a bug in a rug." Spinning on his heel, Sweet Lou stalked out of the freezer and padlocked the door.

Jessica smoothed the hair from Dancer's face and waited for her to regain consciousness. "This is going to be a long night," she mumbled as she quietly began to cry.

DOSED

The moon had just settled over the city when the California Kid came to. She lay unmoving in the darkness, listening for the fall of footsteps, her ears straining for the slightest sound. "I've got to get out of here," the Kid thought as she hastily fumbled through her pockets for a piece of gum. Closing her eyes, and dosed with enough terror and excitement to last two lifetimes, the Kid felt miserable. Clasping her hands between her thighs and turning over on her side, she sifted through some of the facts. Dancer and Jessica were prisoners somewhere. Sweet Lou was on the loose. And she was stuck here. The simplest solution was to make a run for it, and try to get back to Ta Jan's. But that was too obvious; someone would be waiting to nail her. The next-best idea was to sit tight and try to find Dancer and Jessica on her own. The Kid drew herself into a ball, pulling up her shirt collar protectively around her neck. She was too tired to search for another hiding place. If Sweet Lou was going to find her, he was going to find her exactly like this.

AWOL

Ta Jan dipped her croissant into her coffee and stared out past the railing of the deck into the apartment complex across the way. Dancer and the Kid had failed to return. Before they had left, they had not thought to prearrange an emergency signal, and now Ta Jan wondered if their cover had been blown.

Killer Shep stood up and stretched. "And what do you think?" asked Ta Jan.

"Well," Killer Shep said, scratching behind her ear, "it looks bad."

Ta Jan poured herself another cup of coffee. "It's a damn good thing we're going up there today," she said.

"Knock off the 'we' business," growled Killer Shep.

"Oh, come over here, motorcycle ears," Ta Jan purred. "Come here and humor me."

Killer Shep reluctantly trotted over to Ta Jan. She knew what was coming next.

"I need you to guard the wagon, and to be an—"

"Alert, intelligent watchdog. Haven't I bathed you, and fed

you, and kept you from the cold? The baying of the hounds? The howling of the wolves? Haven't I?" Killer Shep's eyes glazed over.

Ta Jan flicked her ear. "OK, you can stop mimicking me now," she sighed. "But it's all true, every last word."

Killer Shep turned aside and guffawed privately. She was getting a little long in the tooth for these speeches.

Ta Jan opened the refrigerator and patted the tuna. Everything seemed in order. "We're leaving in an hour, so don't make yourself too scarce," she said over her shoulder.

Killer Shep curled up in a corner. The thought of accompanying Ta Jan sickened her. Perhaps she could conveniently lose her lunch on the priceless Oriental rug, or beg off with a sudden arthritic attack.

Ta Jan slammed the refrigerator door. "Don't even think it," she yelled. "Or you'll really be in the doghouse."

PERPETUATE

Dancer regained consciousness in the middle of the night. A large knot had formed over right temple, and a searing pain filled her head. Slowly looking about, trying to focus on something familiar, Dancer realized that she had no idea where she was. Reaching out, she touched the sleeping Jessica and shook her gently. "Jessica, babe," she whispered. "Babe."

"Mmmmmmm," replied Jessica, who had been dreaming of sweating horses, open plains, and the California Kid. "God, Dancer, is that you?" she gasped, bolting upright. "I was so worried, I didn't know what to do except make you feel as comfortable as possible."

"I'm in so much pain," exclaimed Dancer. "My head feels like it can barely sit on my shoulders, and every time I attempt to move I slosh my way through an exploding minefield. Jesus, I even have a touch of double vision."

"No, you don't," soothed Jessica calmly. "Here, hon, put these on," she said, handing Dancer her silver rimmed glasses. "They flew off your face when Sweet Lou hit you, and I salvaged them from further damage."

"Bless you, bless you," Dancer cried, smothering her glasses gratefully with kisses. "Where in the hell are we?"

Jessica paused thoughtfully before answering. Not wishing to nauseate the ex-vegetarian, she replied, "An abandoned storage locker."

Dancer frowned. This information contributed a cornflake of knowledge to her already diminished capacity. Turning ever so carefully, she planted a kiss on Jessica's mouth. "Are you hurt?," she tenderly asked, running her fingers over Jessica's lips.

"I've got several small cuts on the inside of my mouth, but basically I'm all right. I'm shaken, but all right," Jessica said, leaning back and cradling Dancer's head against her shoulder.

Dancer lay quietly in Jessica's arms. It was no small wonder they were still alive. The trick, now, was to perpetuate that condition until help arrived. "Hey," she said, nudging Jessica.

"Mmmmmmmmm."

"I need a codeine."

"Hahaha."

"I'm serious."

"Ok, dear, I'll pull on my pantyhose, and dart off to the nearest drugstore."

"Ah, that word."

"What word? Pantyhose?"

"Drugstore."

Jessica locked her arms around Dancer. "How do you suppose the Kid is?"

"Counting sheep somewhere, I imagine."

"Mmmm. I hope she's got a plan."

"Me too," yawned Dancer, slipping away into the night.

SHOWTIME

The Kid woke trembling with fatigue. Her lower back ached, and she was hungry. Stumbling blindly across the room, she found the light switch and flicked it on. The light hurt her eyes and she moved among the cables searching for her backpack. "I need these damn cookies, now," she pleaded, beating back cartons and reams of paper. Tripping over a pile of cassettes, the Kid fell against a stack of boxes. There, lodged like a jewel in the waste, land, was her backpack. Hastily turning off the light, the Kid walked back among the shipping crates and unzipped her back, pack. She dove in and stuffed herself with chocolate chip cookies. This did not lessen her desire for eggs, a rasher of bacon, and home fries. It did, however, give her a substantial sugar rush while her mind anxiously raced around in circles. The Kid sat in the dark and cocked her ear towards the door. "I guess this is it," she said, standing up. "Showtime."

STYLE

Fatin Satin Aspen, plagued by insomnia, took a handful of Valium to quell his blistering mind. For hours, he had lain awake in bed, fearful that Jessica's missing friend would come crashing through his bedroom door, or worse still, sabotage his carefully designed plans. That Dancer and Jessica were prisoners gave him only a fleeting moment of security; he was no fool. He knew they would have to be eliminated as unobtrusively as possible. An accident on the highway? A boating mishap? As much as he admired the turmoil and violence of the Cosa Nostra, Fatin Satin Aspen would not have his hands soiled by gangland-style executions. He was a cut above that. Dancer and Jessica need not fear the assassin's bullet. They would go out in style.

TRUCKING

Ta Jan packed her catering truck with fillet knives, cutting boards, an assortment of dishes, two pounds of fresh Hawaiian tuna, a pound of yellowfin tuna, a tin of Wasabi powder, and various other culinary paraphernalia. Whistling for Killer Shep, she waited patiently behind the wheel while the old dog meandered down the sidewalk. Climbing into the front seat, Killer Shep stuck her nose out the window. Ta Jan sensed that the dog was upset and reached over to scratch Killer Shep's ear. The dog leaned away from her. "So, that's the way it is, huh?" said Ta Jan, out of the side of her mouth. "Aren't you even interested in the game plan?"

"Cram it," snarled the dog as they approached the campus.

"There's the old eucalyptus grove and the Spanish steps," remarked Ta Jan excitedly as they drove up the hill. "Remember how you used to frolic and wait for me along this stretch, between classes?"

The dog's ears perked up. Those had been the best days of her life. As the reigning campus mascot, she had been treated by the kitchen night crew to a daily supper of choice prime rib gristle and scraps. Killer Shep licked her chops as Ta Jan parked the car.

"I hate to add to your morose mood," said Ta Jan, "but over there next to the line of sedans and station wagons is the Kid's limo. So, whether you like it or not, we're up to our elbows in commitment. Do what you like. If you get restless, take a trot around the campus." Ta Jan rolled down the windows of her truck and hoped her words did not fall on deaf ears. Rubbing the dog's head for luck, she rang the doorbell.

Killer Shep lay down in the front seat. She wanted to spare herself the ordeal of making eye contact with Fatin Satin Aspen. Besides, this was Ta Jan's gig, and Killer Shep was only here for the ride.

SITTING DUCKS

Dancer and Jessica awakened to a battery of assorted maladies. Jessica's mouth had puffed up during the night, and her lips had dried and cracked along the outer edges. Dancer's head, still smarting from Sweet Lou's blow, throbbed with every motion.

"How did you sleep?" Dancer asked, pressing the lower muscles of her back.

"Not very well," Jessica replied. "I kept fantasizing the door flying open and Sweet Lou marching us to the underside of the school, where we would be lined up against a wall and executed. Other than that, my back aches, my rib cage is no longer joined to my body, and I feel tired and old."

Dancer took Jessica's hand and squeezed it. Her spirits were dragging and she had nothing to offer in the way of hope except the shadowy figure of the California Kid. "We're going to make it, Babe," Dancer said determinedly, "but if I have to sleep on this floor one more night my bones are going to rise up and revolt."

"Oh, Dancer, you never liked camping, did you?" Jessica laughed.

"I'm glad you find my remark humorous, but this sawdust belongs in a stable. I'm starving, and I don't like sitting here in the dark, and I'd give anything for a strong cup of coffee and to see the Kid's face in the door."

"So would I," Jessica sighed. "Do you think they'll hold us here much longer?"

"Well, the longer we're here the better our chances are for survival. It gives us time to devise some kind of plan. I don't want to go down like a sitting duck."

"Neither do I. But the fact is we know a lot."

"We know too much!"

A cloudburst of silence showered the room, as Dancer and Jessica realized the gravity of their situation.

LINE

The California Kid exited cautiously from the video room. Her mind, rotating the way a weathervane drifts in a fickle wind, entertained thoughts of escape and capture; violence and mayhem. It became increasingly clear to her, as she proceeded, that the road to deliverance meant leaving the campus and seeking help. What good was it, she reasoned, if she tried to find Dancer and Jessica and got captured in the process? Then they would all be three peas in the same pod. The Kid slowly moved down the tunnel path. Her heart was in her mouth as she approached every turn. She had originally thought to leave by the same route she and Dancer had inadvertently discovered: through the wine cellar and into the main building. But her nerves, on the verge of a major collapse, wilted at the thought of making another long run through the tunnel. Worse still, there was the torturous return climb up the winding staircase. As risky as crossing the rose garden presented itself to be, the Kid realized she would have to put her ass on the line and chance it.

MELON

When Sweet Lou unlocked all the locks and opened the door, he was startled by Ta Jan's reflecting sunglasses. Ta Jan, in turn, was startled by his immense physique. Taking note of the number of double locks, bolts, and security chains, she scrutinized Sweet Lou as he escorted her down the hallway. He showed no ill effects or traces of narcotic hangover. This worried Ta Jan.

Deciding to probe his mental capacities, she fed him the oldest line in the book. "You know, you look very familiar. Did you ever play pro ball?"

Sweet Lou's ego swelled to the size of a casaba melon. "Well," he began, "I went to training camp as a free agent with the New York Jets when Namath was still around, and made the team as a second string lineman. That was in '70, '71."

"No kidding," said Ta Jan. "I'm very impressed. Making the team as a free agent takes guts. I knew there was an air of familiarity about you. Did you play long?"

Sweet Lou looked down at Ta Jan and shoveled it on. "Let's see, three seasons before a knee injury side-lined me permanently," he replied. The truth was, in his second year Sweet Lou was waived from the squad because he was overweight and couldn't cut the mustard. In one game alone, opposing linemen rushed his position and blindsided Namath four times. By the end of the exhibition season, Sweet Lou was gone.

Ta Jan absorbed all the information with a grain of salt. The truth was irrelevant, The casualness of the dialogue cautioned her. If Sweet Lou was lying, he was very good at it, and this was something to remember when the sparks began to fly.

REFLECTION

Sweet Lou escorted Ta Jan into Fatin Satin Aspen's office and closed the door after her. Slipping into a side-room, he spoke softly into an intercom. "She's in your office, boss."

"Good, good," came the low reply.

Ta Jan crossed the room and lifted her sunglasses for a closer look at the rose that adorned Fatin Satin Aspen's desk. Blood red, the petals hugged each other in a knot of color above the sterling vase. Leaning over, Ta Jan detected a light fragrance which was pleasing to the senses. As she moved slowly about the room, she was struck by the simplicity of the decor. A large desk, several chairs, a martial arts mat and a full length mirror were the extent of the furnishings. Ta Jan glanced at herself in front of the mirror. A spot on the front of her shirt caught her eye. Annoyed by this, she stopped to rub it.

"Goddamn it," Fatin Satin Aspen cursed when he saw Ta Jan's reflective sunglasses, "how I hate those fucking things."

He was beside himself with disappointment. One of his favorite ploys, which he referred to as the trickle down effect, consisted of staring at a person until the subject melted like a popsicle on a stick. Still smarting from their previous phone conversation, Fatin Satin Aspen could hardly wait to use it on Ta Jan, and now watching her behind the two way mirror, he felt as if the rug had been pulled out from under him. "Oh well," he thought, as he moved towards his office, "we'll just have to work around those dark glasses."

HIP POCKET

While Dancer fitfully slept off her headache, Jessica sat next to her trying to remember where she had left her last will and testament. Always a practical girl, Jessica had written her first will when she was thirteen, leaving her entire rock collection to her parents. Instilled with a sense of order and continuity, and wanting her passing to be as smooth as silk, Jessica was beginning to realize this was not the usual order of the universe as she racked her brains for the will's location.

Frustrated, Jessica stretched out on the floor and began to do pushups while her mind reeled out a litany of regrets. She regretted the day she joined the Brigade. She regretted all the sweaters she had ever knitted in the name of Violia Vincente. She stripped herself of her emissary title, and she accepted full responsibility for their present situation.

An uneasy feeling gripped Jessica as a low rumbling swept through the meat locker. Clutching Dancer's arm, she shouted, "earthquake," as the ground shifted beneath them.

"God," said Dancer hysterically, after the tremors had subsided, "we don't have to worry about Fatin Satin Aspen. We're going to be victims of a natural disaster. And fifty years from now we'll be unearthed as mummies in a pyramid."

Jessica slowly inhaled, and brushed the sawdust from her clothes. "Dancer, I'm sorry," she said.

"Sorry?"

"For all this. For being so vulnerable."

Dancer's heart did a cartwheel through the gloom. Trying to sound matter of fact, she said, "If they bring in the Kid, then we can all sit around and be sorry. Until then," she shrugged, "I'll place your 'sorry' in my hip pocket so you can stroke it every now and then."

Jessica smiled. Sometimes, Dancer could be so distractingly coy. Leaning back into the sawdust, Jessica wondered where the Kid was and what the odds were on their being rescued before another earthquake struck.

MMV

Ta Jan sat opposite Fatin Satin Aspen and stared at him through her dark glasses. He hadn't changed much since their first encounter, a little grayer perhaps, heavier from years of indulgence, he oozed a certain paternal self-confidence.

Fatin Satin Aspen rolled a smile across his lips. His stomach, peppered with Maalox, knotted in frustration as Ta Jan's glasses mockingly spit back his image. "At last, my dear, this is a thrill. If I seemed a bit aggressive in our phone conversation it was merely my desire to hire your services which carried me away. I hope you will forgive my rudeness."

Ta Jan nodded her head. "I accept your apology. Sometimes the situation dictates the action. Now, tell me a little about this dinner you are hosting."

Fatin Satin Aspen shifted in his chair. He unfolded his hands and placed them on top of the desk. "You have heard of the Bohemian Club?"

"Yes," Ta Jan replied, her eyes narrowing behind the dark glasses.

"I am planning to invite several clusters of the membership to a post-Bohemian weekend dinner. As you probably know, our gathering takes place in a month, which leaves little time for preparation. The theme of the dinner will be California wines. Therefore, the various courses should enhance the featured vintages."

"Don't you think it should be the other way around? One, does not, after all build a city without a blueprint."

"Ah, yes, but many a city has been planned around a river. And that's what I foresee. I want the evening to focus expressly on those wines. And I want the appetizers and entrees to spring up like glittering cities along a waterway."

"Well done," thought Ta Jan. "What vineyards are you planning to showcase? There are several I am quite familiar with. Perhaps, we could compare lists?"

"No need for that," Fatin Satin Aspen brusquely responded. "I plan to feature my own label."

"Which is?"

"MMV."

Ta Jan gagged on the information. MMV was an overpriced label which she found undrinkable. "This seems like a rather ambitious endeavor," she said. "I need time to think this offer through. If I accept, you can be reassured of my full commitment."

Fatin Satin Aspen leapt to his feet. "Well," he said pleasantly, repressing his desire to shatter Ta Jan's glasses, "take all the time you need. And now, some lunch?"

Ta Jan stood up. "Since I suggested lunch, I thought it only fair that I provide it. Perhaps your assistant can open the front door?"

Fatin Satin Aspen rang for Sweet Lou. Ta Jan's generosity overwhelmed him. He was planning to serve chicken salad sandwiches on rye.

Ta Jan gleefully eyed her host. She wondered if he had eaten a large breakfast. Her game plan depended on it.

ACE

Killer Shep picked up Ta Jan's scent as she approached the catering wagon. Sitting up, she caught a glimpse of a huge figure standing in the shadow of the doorway. Shivering, Killer Shep slipped back down into the safety of the front seat as Ta Jan unloaded several containers from the van.

"Well, biscuit breath," Ta Jan said, "we're on first base, and hopefully aided by the simplicity of this lunch, we'll soon be moseying home."

"I don't buy any of that."

"Any of what?"

"Any of your optimism."

"Really," Ta Jan said, "you forgot, I always have an ace up my sleeve."

"What? What do you have that I don't know about?"

"You'll see."

"That's just it, I don't want to."

Ta Jan slammed the back door. "One more thing," she said,

as she passed the side of the car, "keep an eye out for the Kid and Dancer."

Killer Shep grunted and lay with her head jutting over the front seat. Her mind tossed and turned. Ta Jan's plan was the last straw. Sitting up and staring out across the campus, Killer Shep was overcome with nostalgia. She hopped through the window, and trotted peacefully towards a clump of daffodils.

DEPOSIT

The Kid crept along the building wall, which ended at the rose garden. Nervous and sweaty, she slowly poked her head through an opening in the hedge. What she saw made her smile in all the right places. Who would have thought that the sight of an old German shepherd peeing in the freesias could cause all the commotion that zigzagged through the Kid's heart.

"Pssst, Killer," whispered the Kid wiping her face with the back of her hand.

Killer Shep's lips curled upward. Her mouth dropped into a smile. Sniffing her way through the roses, she daintily deposited last night's Alpo at the base of Fatin Satin Aspen's sterling silver hybrids, and disappeared into the hedges just as the earthquake shimmied across the lawn.

TALASARU

Ta Jan spread a linen cloth across Fatin Satin Aspen's desk. Upon this she placed a pair of ivory chopsticks, two small plates, and a dish of wasabi paste. Reaching into her basket, she uncovered a platter of exquisitely arranged sushi. The iridescent texture of seaweed, wrapped around pearls of rice, raw tuna and vegetable slivers, swam before Fatin Satin Aspen's eyes like a cluster of precious gems. His taste buds ballooned with anticipation. He could barely contain himself.

"May I?" he stuttered, his chopsticks poised hungrily in midair.

"Absolutely," Ta Jan replied, bringing forth a cutting board, three fillet knives, and two slabs of raw tuna.

"This," said Ta Jan pointing to a crimson mass, "is fresh Hawaiian tuna, and this is Pacific yellow fin." Choosing a slender knife adorned with a rosewood handle, Ta Jan sliced deftly through the tuna. Stacking the sashimi like ruby chips along the board, she presented a full plate to Fatin Satin Aspen.

Fatin Satin Aspen mixed a dollop of the wasabi paste with a dash of soy sauce. He had already knocked off half the plate of sushi, and he was now girding himself for more serious consumptions. Dipping a sashimi morsel into the wasabi, Fatin Satin Aspen transferred it to his watering mouth. A smile broke across his face as his nostrils flared and his eyes filled with tears. "Splendid," he gasped. "You are not joining me?"

"Not until I finish slicing the rest of these," said Ta Jan. "Believe me, my reward is watching you."

Fatin Satin Aspen smiled to himself. How fortunate he was to be served like this. He made a mental note to recruit more Asian labor.

A rush of adrenalin poured through Ta Jan as Fatin Satin Aspen polished off the platter of sushi, and the first plate of sashimi. "How easy it would be to reach across the desk and slit his throat," she thought as she carefully arranged the yellow fin tuna. "Just out of curiosity," she asked, "what were you going to serve me?"

Fatin Satin Aspen, cheapskate of cheapskates, tried to cover his tight ass by replying, "Steak and lobster."

A slight smile flickered across Ta Jan's face. He was not half the liar that Sweet Lou was. "You know," she began, stopping suddenly as the dishes on the desk jumped and clattered, and the floor rolled, "earthquake!"

Fatin Satin Aspen clutched the edge of his desk as the San Andreas fault line pitched back and forth for several seconds. "Not me. Not now," he pleaded, his heart pounding rapidly, as his beard bunched up in waves against the desk.

Ta Jan, crouched anxiously in front of her chair, cautiously lifted her head as the tremors slowly ceased.

"Jesus," Fatin Satin Aspen muttered, "I hate living in this goddamn state."

"Somewhat like Russian roulette, wouldn't you say?" replied Ta Jan sitting back down in her chair.

Fatin Satin Aspen grunted. He had suddenly lost his appetite for food and for conversation. Looking over at Ta Jan he said, "Forgive my haste, but within the next hour I have several pressing engagements which I must prepare for." Reflecting on the delicacies he had consumed, he added, "You are to be commended for the simplicity of the meal."

Ta Jan slowly nodded, and removed her dark glasses. "You are currently in possession of something I want."

Fatin Satin Aspen rose from his chair. "Oh?"

"Two unlucky intruders."

Fatin Satin Aspen sat back down and fastened his eyes on Ta Jan. "That's a peculiar request," he slowly said.

"Let's not insult each other's intelligence," Ta Jan said, placing her cards on the table. "My two friends, for the antidote to the poison which is circulating through your digestive tract."

Fatin Satin Aspen's pulse skipped a beat. "Don't try and hustle me," he calmly said. "Do you know who I am?" he hissed.

"In the South Pacific islands, there is a fish called Talasaru which is considered a delicacy. It is unfortunately highly toxic and often fatal to humans when improperly prepared. There are only twelve master chefs in the country who are certified to serve this fish. I," said Ta Jan coldly, "am not one of them. The first round of sashimi was Talasaru. You are slowly dying."

Fatin Satin Aspen stroked his beard. "My dear, we're six thousand miles from the South Pacific. Do you really expect me to believe I was served this poisonous fish?"

Ta Jan put her dark glasses back on, and shrugged her shoulders.

Fatin Satin Aspen reached across the desk and ripped the glasses off Ta Jan's face. "This," he roared, snapping the glasses in two, "is how I'm going to break you and your pals."

LOAD

Sweet Lou was knitting a pale green muffler when the phone call came through. "Get your butt up here, now," bellowed a familiar voice.

"Right-o, boss," replied Sweet Lou as he put away his knitting needles and cleared his chair of wool. Folding the partially knitted muffler into a plastic bag, Sweet Lou stuffed his locker and slammed the door. His afternoon had been ruined. Worn out by the futile search for the Kid, Sweet Lou had looked forward to the mandatory three-hour stint in the sewing circle.

Slipping into a vacant stall in the men's room, Sweet Lou carefully unwrapped a rectangular piece of paper. "Well," he pouted, sucking up a load of cocaine through a red and white plastic straw, "at least I have this."

BAD ROLL

Killer Shep's head leaned into the Kid's knee as the Kid affectionately thumped the shepherd's side. It was clear that a bond had started to form between them. Killer Shep had informally adopted the Kid into her pack, and the Kid, longing for companionship, was drawn to the affable, street-wise canine.

"I'm so glad to see you, girl," exclaimed the Kid as she scratched the Shepherd under her chin. "It's been a nightmare. Dancer and her girlfriend are locked up. This place is controlled by castoffs from the NFL, and a place called the Napa Valley is about to be extinguished. You've got to help me get out of here."

Killer Shep whistled to herself. Never have so few been involved with so much. She cocked her head and looked pensively at the Kid.

The Kid slung her backpack off her shoulders, and rummaged for a piece of gum. Anxiety shot through her system as her hand frantically crisscrossed the bag. Dropping the bag on the ground, the Kid patted herself down. "Oh god," she cried, "I'm gumless!"

Killer Shep scratched her ear. She was dismayed by the Kid's helplessness.

So was the Kid as black dots swarmed before her eyes. Clutching Killer Shep's coat, she gasped, "I'm going to faint, again."

Killer Shep followed the Kid's gaze. A colony of ants scurried back and forth across the ground. "This is beyond the call of duty," the shepherd thought, as she jumped on top of the Kid and sent her sprawling to the ground.

"Ants?" the Kid quizzically murmured. "Ants!" she sheepishly exclaimed, swatting several dozen off her knee. "You see how this gum withdrawal business works," the Kid nervously said. "The mind plays nasty tricks on reality." The Kid stood up and dusted her pant legs off. "Wait a minute!" she cried as her gray matter went into overdrive. "You're here with me. And I'm with you. Where's Ta Jan?"

Killer Shep's tail began to wag. Her tail always wagged at the sound of Ta Jan's name. Backing out from the confines of the hedges she grinned, turned once to look at the Kid, and padded across the garden.

The Kid, gumless and on a bad roll, watched in disbelief as the next best thing to vanilla bean ice cream walked away from her. "Wait," she yelled. "For chrissake, wait for me."

Killer Shep flipped back her ears. She knew the Kid expected her to lead them to Ta Jan. That was the least of her intentions. She wondered how long it would take the Kid to realize that she was barking up the wrong tree.

ESCALATION

Fatin Satin Aspen's eyes riveted Ta Jan to her chair. She was no match for the cold fixed stare that held her in place. Concentrating on the rose petals to her left, Ta Jan focused her eyes on a spot directly behind Fatin Satin Aspen's head. Fatin Satin Aspen shifted in his chair. She was good. But he was better.

When Sweet Lou entered the room, he thought he could hear a pin drop.

Without taking his eyes off Ta Jan, Fatin Satin Aspen said, "I want you to put her on ice with her friends. Then, I want you to come back here to discuss your flight instructions."

"OK, boss," Sweet Lou replied, grabbing Ta Jan by the wrist and pushing her in front of him.

"By the way, you *have* finished your search, haven't you?"

Sweet Lou stopped dead in his tracks. "Hours ago, boss," he deadpanned. "You can sleep tight tonight."

"Good. Good," Fatin Satin Aspen murmured, waving them out of the room. Standing behind his desk, he patted his belly. A small wave of nausea tickled his esophagus. Indigestion, he reassured himself. "Jesus," he thought, "if I listened to all the things everyone had ever planted in my mind I'd be a fucking paranoid." Stroking his beard, Fatin Satin Aspen realized the situation was escalating. The meat locker was quickly filling with enemies. He would have to act swiftly.

REVELATIONS

Dancer and Jessica were caught off guard by Ta Jan's arrival. The door burst open, and Ta Jan's body flew in. "So much for an escape plan," cracked an embarrassed Dancer, as she moved slowly to embrace Ta Jan.

"Welcome," said Jessica warmly, shaking Ta Jan's hand and leading her to a corner of the room.

"I'm sorry that you're a part of this," Dancer said. "But I have to be truthful and say that I'm glad to see you, even under these circumstances."

Ta Jan reached out and patted Dancer's shoulder. In the dim light, Dancer and Jessica's figures were barely distinguishable, but judging from the manner in which Dancer cautiously moved, Ta Jan knew they had probably suffered some physical mishaps. Ta Jan closed her eyes, and rubbed her temples. "What exactly is going on here?" she asked calmly.

Jessica crossed her legs and hunched forward. Picking up a handful of sawdust, she dribbled it through her fingers. "Ever hear of 2,4,5-T?"

Ta Jan drew in a breath. "Most certainly. During the Vietnam War, 2,4,5-T combined with 2,4-D formed the toxic Agent Orange, which was used by the army to defoliate the jungles of Vietnam. Now 2,4,5-T is thought to have been responsible for numerous birth mishaps and cancer-related deaths."

Jessica shivered as a cold wave of fear enveloped her body. "Let me tell you a story," Ta Jan continued. "After the Army had completed their various Agent Orange runs, and the trees had been successfully defoliated, the Vietnamese people, trying very basically to survive, would systematically cut down the trees, and use the wood as fuel."

Dancer groaned. The revelations sickened her as she imagined herself cooking food over kindling which had been sprayed with a toxin like Agent Orange. Her voice shook with rage as she recounted Fatin Satin Aspen's plans for the Napa Valley, and for Jessica.

Ta Jan listened silently and added the information to the

facts she already knew. "Where's the Kid?" she urgently inquired.

Dancer placed her hand on Ta Jan's knee. "We don't know," she gloomily said. "Hopefully, regrouping and enlisting aid."

Ta Jan turned to Jessica. "Is there a physician in residence?"

"No, but there's an infirmary, and a nurse on call. Actually, I think Fatin Satin Aspen considers himself quite the medical layman. Rumor has it that he has access to a wide range of pharmaceutical supplies. Why?"

"Because in about half an hour Fatin Satin Aspen is going to be in dire need of medical attention." Ta Jan paused dramatically. "I poisoned him."

"You what!" shouted Dancer.

"Well, I didn't actually poison him. But I want him to think I did. I mixed in mannite, an Italian baby laxative with which cocaine is sometimes cut, to the wasabi mixture I gave him. His symptoms, nausea, cramps, and a bad case of the trots, are close enough to those associated with a poisoning."

Dancer howled in disbelief. The thought of Fatin Satin Aspen mired in his own cesspool rocked her body with laughter. Jessica, clutching her heaving sides, shrieked into the sawdust. "Where I come from," she hiccoughed, "we'd call you plenty akamai."

"And where might that be, tita?" shot back a surprised Ta Jan.

Jessica's head bolted upright as she recognized the singsong pidgin English of her beloved Hawaiian Islands. "Oh no," she giggled.

"Oh yes," confirmed Ta Jan, breaking out into a new wave of laughter which consumed Jessica as well. "I've lived on the mainland for close to fifteen years, now, and never have I met anyone else who was born and raised in the islands."

"This must be your lucky day," interjected Dancer soberly. "We hope the same can be said for our blue-eyed Kid."

"Hear, hear," added Jessica quickly, her heart skipping a beat at the thought of the Kid lying in some section of the tunnel with her head bashed in and bleeding.

TENPINS

Killer Shep padded along the perimeter of the rose garden, stopping occasionally to water the lawn and sniff a lavender bush or two. Concerned not only for the Kid's welfare but for her own safety, she skirted the main thoroughfare and kept to the paths which circled the hillside of the campus. The Kid followed in silence, filled with the hope that the shepherd was leading them to Ta Jan. This, however, was not what Killer Shep had in mind. Remembering the lunch freebies, and the T-bone scraps of yesteryear, overwhelmed by nostalgia and sentimentality, Killer Shep wound her way along the hillside until she was directly below the back door of the kitchen. Creeping up through the bushes, they hid behind a towering brick incinerator at the edge of the hill. "Is she in there, girl? Is that where Ta Jan is?" asked the Kid, pointing to the slate walls of the cafeteria. "Well," she commanded, "go get her."

The shepherd tilted her head and gazed soberly at the Kid. Did she have a surprise coming!

The Kid whacked the shepherd on the rump, and watched as the old dog trotted slowly towards the building. Five feet from the door, the shepherd stopped abruptly. Circling and sniffing several large trash cans, she knocked them over like tenpins in a bowling alley.

The Kid went wild with rage. Where was the dog when they passed out the brains?

Killer Shep, scarfing her way through mounds of debris, had only a split second to dodge the charging Kid, who hooked several fingers around her collar and yanked her angrily from the feast.

The shepherd howled.

Twenty-five feet away, in the meat locker, Ta Jan jumped to her feet, and ran towards the door.

TUNA FISH AND BAGATELLE

Fatin Satin Aspen, wandering dreamily around in his cavernous ego waiting patiently for Sweet Lou, who was stuffing his face with Lorna Doones at the arcade vending machines, was standing before a large window overlooking the parking lot when he experienced acute abdominal pain. His hands went cold, and his brain cells clung frantically to each other as he remembered Ta Jan's threat. Doubled over, and pale as a bucket of bones, Fatin Satin Aspen deposited himself in the nearest restroom. His system under full siege tried to make short work of the mannite filtering through his intestines. But the tuna fish which he so gluttonously devoured, much like the offense of a football team, had to compete against a sluggish defensive line consisting of scrambled eggs, sausages, and blueberry muffins. The tuna fish moved slowly down the field against the stalwart breakfast line. Fatin Satin Aspen placed his head between his knees—not an easy maneuver for a person of his stature in a crapper the size of a shoebox. The tuna fish quarterback rolled out, sending up a wave of nausea; "I'm fucking dying," screamed Fatin Satin Aspen as an ocean of sweat cascaded down his forehead into his beard. The stick-to-your-ribs breakfast lobbed up a blueberry muffin. Then another. Fatin Satin Aspen forced himself to stand. Resembling a sack of potatoes in a shopping cart, he pushed open the door and reeled down the hallway to his office. Picking up the phone on his desk, he dialed the infirmary and told the nurse, Bagatelle, to get her ass over to his office. "I've been fucking poisoned," he croaked, collapsing in a heap on the polished floor.

Nurse Bagatelle flipped a bennie down her gullet and filled her satchel with smelling salts, vinegar, raw eggs, and an armful of medical supplies. Pulling on her white pantyhose, she straightened her RN pin and ran through the building. This was Bagatelle's first emergency. From the moment Fatin Satin Aspen hired her she disliked him. But even though the pay was lousy she stuck it out, attracted by the free room and board, and the various medicinal perks. Nurse Bagatelle neared Fatin Satin Aspen's office. She hoped his illness was something simple like the flu, or indigestion, ailments that could easily be remedied, because she really wasn't a nurse. The RN pin belonged to her dead sister, Brigette. And the only medical experience Bagatelle had was as a teen-age candy striper.

DIGITS

Ta Jan put her fingers between her teeth and whistled. The shepherd's ears stood up like flag poles. The Kid, dragging

Killer Shep from the garbage pile, was surprised to feel the dog go momentarily limp. About to say, "That's more like it," she felt the shepherd jerk her head sharply back, and slip her collar. The Kid swore furiously as Killer Shep dashed towards a small rectangular building set apart from all the others. Scratching the door, her tail rotating like a pinwheel on a stick, Killer Shep waited patiently as the Kid trudged over to her.

"I told you I had an ace, didn't I," Ta Jan called slyly through the door.

"Who, me?" the dog astonishedly replied, knowing full well it had been her all along. Killer Shep leaned against the door.

"What in hell are you up to?" muttered the Kid.

"Kid?" called Ta Jan.

"Ta Jan? Ta Jan!" cried the Kid, her voice somersaulting through the air.

"Listen carefully," said Ta Jan, "I'm here with Dancer and Jessica."

"Are they all right?"

"They're fine," Ta Jan calmly replied.

"There's a combination lock on the door," noted the Kid.

"I know. I suggest that we try to crack the combination. We have nothing to lose."

"It's too crazy," said the Kid. "I'm not going to consider it."

"Look, we know the digits have to be a simple, memorable, 1, 2, 3, combination. Well, will you at least try it?"

"Please," said a voice which the Kid knew to be Jessica's.

"All right," the Kid pouted. After fiddling with different sequences, she frustratedly threw up her hands. "This isn't cutting it. I have a better idea, but you're going to have to sit tight for a while longer. Can you manage?"

"Hey, Kid," called Dancer, "do whatever it takes."

The Kid grinned and flipped the padlock on its hinges. "Let's go," she said to Killer Shep as she turned and scrambled down the hill.

RESURRECTION

Bagatelle found Fatin Satin Aspen lying next to his desk. His face, devoid of color, rose from the twisted ruins of his beard like an enormous egg. Gingerly, Bagatelle stepped over Fatin Satin Aspen's body. She knelt beside him and placed her fingers on his wrist.

Fatin Satin Aspen's eyes flew open.

Bagatelle screamed.

"What the hell's wrong with this nurse?" thought Fatin Satin Aspen.

"You goddamn son of a bitch, weak tickers run in the family," cursed Bagatelle, momentarily forgetting who she was addressing and why she was there.

Fatin Satin Aspen rose up on one elbow. He was a dying man about to commit his first murder. "Help me," he snapped, "or I swear on my dead mother's grave, as my last act, I'll kick your can out the window."

Bernadette Bagatelle looked out the windows behind Fatin Satin Aspen's desk and pulled herself together. Tossing her hair back over her shoulders, she felt Fatin Satin Aspen's pulse and took his temperature. His skin, covered with a light film of perspiration, felt cold as she swabbed his forehead with a piece of gauze.

"What's my temperature?" whispered Fatin Satin Aspen.

"Thank god, it's normal," Bagatelle shuddered, reaching into her satchel and handing Fatin Satin Aspen a bottle of Kaopectate. "Drink this," she ordered.

Fatin Satin Aspen screwed up his face and drank half the bottle. "This tastes like shit," he complained.

Bagatelle cracked two eggs into a glass, and mixed it with a slug of vinegar. "Down the hatch with this," she said, giving him the cloudy mixture.

"THIS TASTES LIKE SHIT TOO."

"Now," said Bagatelle ignoring his remark, "I want you to try to walk around the room. We must get those fluids circulating."

For the first time in his life, Fatin Satin Aspen did as he was told. First he crawled. And then he walked. Strange how he didn't feel like a dying man anymore. The presence of Bagatelle, the nurse, gave him a great sense of security.

Bagatelle watched her patient hobble around the room. This was not the figure of a dying man. Perhaps his system had indeed been poisoned, but, lucky for her, it was something she could appear to be knowledgeable about. Wiping the sweat off her upper lip, Bagatelle lit a cigarette.

Fatin Satin Aspen smiled thinly to himself. He felt like the luckiest man on earth.

SHINE

The Kid, hidden from view by a grove of eucalyptus trees, patiently watched the parking lot for signs of unusual activity. Crouched behind the trunk of one large tree, she picked up a handful of eucalyptus pods and shook them next to Killer Shep's ear.

"This is the plan," she said to the dog who lay in a bed of leaves. "That red car across the way is my car. I need to get several items from the back seat and the trunk. You can help by staying here and being my backup."

Killer Shep panted into the Kid's knee. So far, she liked this plan.

"The moment, and I mean at the *first* sign of any trouble, you are to leap from this grove and save my ass."

Killer Shep licked the Kid's hand. Here was another numbskull who believed all that crap about canine heroics. Over the years, Killer Shep had learned how to shine people on. Wagging her tail, she circled the Kid excitedly. The Kid beamed down at her. When push came to shove, she knew the old dog could be counted on.

TARGET

After his intestinal disruptions had subsided, Fatin Satin Aspen asked Bagatelle to prop him up in his chair. Watching her leave, he made a mental note to send her a bottle of MMV for saving his life. She deserved it. Picking up the phone, he rang for the tardy Sweet Lou.

"Where have you been?" he screamed.

"Nowhere, boss," replied Sweet Lou.

"That's just it. You were supposed to report back to me over an hour ago."

"It totally slipped my mind," Sweet Lou apologized.

"Forget it," rasped Fatin Satin Aspen. "Our plans have changed. You're flying out immediately. So get your ass up here, now, so I can review the map with you."

Sweet Lou put the phone down, raised his fists in the air, and let out a wild whoop. There was nothing he enjoyed more than flying a plane. Not even chocolate chip cookies. Running up three flights of stairs, he burst into Fatin Satin Aspen's office.

Fatin Satin Aspen looked up from his desk. Sweet Lou's mouth hung open like a misshapen bagel. "Gee, boss, you look terrible," Sweet Lou said, cracking his knuckles in anticipation of the flight instructions.

"Yeah, well, that fucking Ta Jan tried to poison me. But as you can see, I'm still here. Now," continued Fatin Satin Aspen, unfolding an aeronautical chart, "this is the topographical map of the Northern California vineyards and the surrounding terrain." Pointing to the Napa Valley region, he said, "You are to start spraying here within this corridor and finish up just outside the valley itself. You will fly a 360 degree circumference until all your tanks are dry. Is that clear?"

"Yeah, boss, perfectly. Now, let me get this straight. I'm to start spraying here," Sweet Lou said, pointing to an area west of the Mayacamas Range which bordered the Napa Valley.

"No, no, dummy, those are my vineyards!"

Fatin Satin Aspen closed his eyes as his entire future flashed before him. Stroking his beard, he slowly opened his eyes. This was the idiot he was placing his fortune in? Picking up a box of red adhesive dots, he peeled off four and stuck them to the map. "Look, my boy, how easy I have made this for you. Spray everything between these dots. Spare nothing. Figure out what the coordinates are, and stick to them. It's as simple as that."

Sweet Lou nodded appreciatively. The boss was the greatest. There was not a chance in hell he could miss the target area. "You're a genius," Sweet Lou said, "a fucking genius."

"I'm glad you recognize that," chuckled Fatin Satin Aspen, folding up the map and placing it in the far corner of his desk. "Before you start loading the drums I want you to do one last errand. Go down to the meat locker and bring me Ta Jan."

BOHEMIANS

Dancer impatiently threw some sawdust across the room. "What in hell is keeping the Kid?" she asked. "My patience is wearing thin."

"Sit on it," exploded Jessica. "Look, it's just as hard for me and Ta Jan as it is for you to be here. Give the Kid a chance. For chrissake, loosen up. We don't need additional stress."

Dancer frowned. "This hasn't exactly been a joy-ride. In case you've forgotten, we're in this up to our necks."

Ta Jan leaned her head back against the wall. What they didn't need was a domestic crisis. "Jessica," she diplomatically said, "what do you know about the Bohemians?"

"The beatniks?"

A smile skidded across Dancer's face. "Honestly, you and the Kid . . ."

"The Bohemians," repeated Ta Jan, severing Dancer's remark before it led to another hostile exchange.

Jessica shrugged her shoulders. "All I know of is Fatin Satin Aspen's connection with them."

"After you," Ta Jan replied, pointing to Dancer, who slowly described the Grove and the Club members.

"So, what you have is a gathering of some of the richest, most powerful men in the country," Jessica said pensively.

"Exactly," nodded Ta Jan.

"I remember hearing a report that back in the sixties Nixon gave the keynote address, and that Ford addressed the group at some point in the seventies," added Dancer.

"I'm beginning to understand this Fatin Satin Aspen more and more," said Ta Jan. "His plan, the defoliation of the major vineyards, would put him in a position through MMV, his vineyard, to dominate the domestic wine scene. And wishing to insure his success, what a better way than, at a formal dinner, serving the surviving California label to some of the nation's most influential men. His partner Alain, I might add, probably handles the oenology end of the business."

"So having attained all this power, Fatin Satin Aspen would be free to pursue any goal he desires," remarked Jessica uneasily.

"Right," continued Ta Jan. "He would no longer be one of the smaller fish in the pond. He would finally garner the world-recognition that the Venerable Brigade has been unable to provide."

"What an imagination."

"What an ego."

"What an asshole," they all chorused in unison.

SKY-HIGH

Sweet Lou twirled the numbers on the combination lock. His mind grappled with the sequences, but happily for him, Fatin

Satin Aspen in his infinite wisdom had chosen the digits 7-11. All Sweet Lou had to do was think of the store, and he would remember the numbers. Pulling down on the lock, he swiveled the latch to one side.

"Freeze," ordered a familiar voice behind him. The faint odor of a burning cigar wafted through the air as Sweet Lou slowly pivoted and faced the Kid.

"You!" he bellowed. "I ought to punch your face in!" he cried as he fumbled for the automatic which hung at his side.

"Uh-uh. Touch that and I'll blow us all into orbit," the Kid said, waving a large packet of dynamite in Sweet Lou's face.

"You're bluffing," Sweet Lou gulped.

"Well," said the Kid sucking on her cigar, "you'll never know until it's too late. And then what? Is anyone going to miss you?"

Sweet Lou held his breath as the Kid's burning cigar hovered over the dangerously short fuse. He didn't know if anyone would miss him. But he knew he would miss flying the plane. On the other hand, if everyone escaped, Fatin Satin Aspen might ring his bell.

Sweet Lou dropped his gun to the ground. The gleam in the Kid's eye meant business. He would rather take his chances with Fatin Satin Aspen than be blown sky-high.

"Now," ordered the Kid, "back it up."

Sweet Lou backpedaled for several feet. A black and tan shepherd slunk out of the shadows and stood to the left of Sweet Lou's ass. Growling menacingly, the shepherd injected a bucketful of fear into his heart.

"Killer, hold him there," the Kid commanded as she picked up the gun. "If he moves one muscle, bite his ass off."

The shepherd nodded.

So did Sweet Lou, who could feel the dog's hot breath on the back of his thigh.

The Kid opened the door. A river of light poured into the darkness as she leaned into the doorway.

ABSURDITIES

Fatin Satin Aspen drummed his fingers on the edge of his desk. He was unhappy with himself. He had violated one of his mother Mary's cardinal rules: Never trust anyone.

"You see, Morris," he could hear his dead mother saying, "it's a miracle you're not six feet under and pushing up daisies. Like me. How could you be such a dope?"

"How could I be such a dope?" Fatin Satin Aspen repeated. "How could I be so trusting? So gullible?"

"That's what you get, Morris," his dead mother chided, "for letting your appetites rule you."

"Enough," swore Fatin Satin Aspen. He clamped his hands over his ears, pushed himself away from his desk, and walked slowly to the full-length mirror. Murder was a nasty business. So was revenge. But how he looked forward to this. For Ta Jan he had something special planned. Plucking his box of scorpions from a desk drawer, he rattled them around in their stony nests. The clock in the tower chimed the hour. Fatin Satin Aspen stroked his beard and gazed restlessly around the room. "Where is that moron?" he muttered. As he stepped into the hallway, a wave of paranoia drenched Fatin Satin Aspen's brain cells.

What if Sweet Lou had been attacked?

By the girls?

Again?

Chuckling nervously at his absurd thoughts, Fatin Satin Aspen headed directly for the rear of the school.

BUSINESS

The Kid led the disheveled band of escapees past the incinerator, around the hillside, and into the grove of eucalyptus trees. Dancer sagged wearily against a tree trunk as the group paused to rest.

"How's your headache, love?" asked Jessica. She ran her fingers through Dancer's hair.

"It's almost gone," lied Dancer, wiping her glasses on Jessica's robe. "Kid," she said, "you haven't told us how you did it."

"Did what?" the Kid modestly replied, her eyes twinkling in the shaded light.

"Well," sighed Dancer, "I'd die happy if I knew how you brought Sweet Lou to heel."

The Kid slung her backpack off her shoulders and tossed a cylindrically shaped bundle to Dancer.

"Emergency road fuses and cigars?" a puzzled Dancer said.

"Dynamite," the Kid solemnly replied.

A stream of grins spread from face to face. Dancer put her arm around the Kid, "You are a wicked bitch," she admiringly said.

"Whoa," said Ta Jan. "We're not out of this until we're home. But I'll tell you this, I can see my van in the parking lot, and it's a wondrous sight."

"Praise God," muttered Killer Shep.

Dancer grabbed the Kid's wrist. "Jessica, you and Killer Shep ride with Ta Jan. The Kid and I have one bit of remaining business to take care of."

"Wait a minute," the Kid cried, breaking free from Dancer. "No. A thousand times no. I'm finished. I've kept my word. I want no part of whatever it is that you have on you mind."

"What the hell is going on here?" shouted Jessica. "We're all leaving together or we're not leaving at all." Ta Jan sighed and pulled Jessica to a neutral corner.

"Please," begged Dancer, turning to the Kid, "one more shot and then it's over. For chrissake, Kid, have a heart, my vision's screwed up and I'm seeing double," she whispered.

The California Kid stubbed the toe of her boot into the ground. "Wipe your goddamn glasses again," she growled, "so you can try to see where it is we're going."

Dancer hugged the Kid gratefully, and kissed a bewildered Jessica. "Everything's going to be all right. You'll see."

Ta Jan shook her head. Not many things were beyond her comprehension. This one was. "See you back at the flat," she said hopefully. "If you're not back in an hour, I'm calling out the troops."

DUNGEON

Fatin Satin Aspen reached the meat locker just as the Kid and Dancer were skulking through his office. Turning the tumblers as fast as fingers would allow, he whipped off the lock and pulled open the door.

Silhouetted against the light, Fatin Satin Aspen looked like Godzilla to Sweet Lou, who walked dejectedly to the center of the room.

Fatin Satin Aspen elevated himself to his full height and stood eyeball to eyeball with Sweet Lou. "Idiot," he screamed. "Simpleton. I sent a boy to do a man's job. Forty days in the dungeon. Forty fucking days."

"Boss," Sweet Lou whispered, "we don't have a dungeon."

"Shut up," thundered Fatin Satin Aspen. "Then forty days cleaning up after the scorpions."

"Not that," shuddered Sweet Lou. "Not the cage."

Fatin Satin Aspen bit his lip. "Leave now, this moment, immediately, on your mission," he ordered. "Let nothing stop you. If you have to piss, do it in your pants. Go down to the cellar, load the containers and head directly for the airport. And for chrissake pick up your flight map in my office. If you bungle this, I swear on my dead mother's grave, your head will roll."

Sweet Lou tiptoed past Fatin Satin Aspen. The blood rushed to his face as his mind looped through the clouds. He didn't feel as bad as he pretended.

CHART

Sweet Lou unfolded the aeronautical map and began to chart his course. Even though the boss's explicit directions to spray all areas between the red dots simplified his calculations, Sweet Lou bent over the table and labored at his task. This was his least favorite part. When he flew in the campaign to eradicate the med-fly, someone always had to assist him with his coordinates. Taking his time, reminding himself of the gravity of the mission, Sweet Lou painstakingly figured his positions. Never one to double-check his work, Sweet Lou then rubbed his hands together and bounded swiftly for the plane.

PROVERB

Waiting for Fatin Satin Aspen in a neat pile on his desk were five long-stem sterling roses which had been severed from their stalks. A scrap of paper lying on top of them read: "May you live a long and interesting life."

Fatin Satin Aspen crumpled the note and swept the roses off his desk. "No doubt those foolish girls," he thought as the tower bells chimed. "Too late for them," he mused. "Too late for anyone. In a little while," he noted, "I shall be the undisputed king of Napa Valley. Number one, Mom," he cried, raising his eyes to the ceiling, and pointing his index finger to the sky. "Number one," he chanted over and over, through his open window, and office door.

Bernadette Bagatelle, returning from the library with an armful of *New England Medical Journals*, listened in amazement as Fatin Satin Aspen's voice leaked out into the corridor. "Holy shit," she murmured, "maybe there's the gift of healing in these hands."

SHOOTING STAR

At approximately 7:15, a blip of unidentifiable origins crisscrossed the radar screens at Travis Air Force Base. Unable to raise a response, the control tower radioed for ground level assistance to the highway patrol. One officer, Chuck E. Chips, sitting in a speed trap off Highway One, crushed out his cigarette and responded to the call.

"This is Officer Charles E. Chips of the highway patrol. I read you, Travis."

"This is Travis. We are tracking a low-flying plane in your vicinity. Can you get a make on this plane? I repeat, can you make it?"

"Negative," replied Officer Chuck E. Chips, "I can hear the S.O.B. but I can't see him."

"Too bad. Too bad," replied Travis. "We're going to intercept this clown and escort him back down. He's in direct violation, I repeat direct violation, of air lanes. Can you take over at touchdown?"

"Affirmative," answered Officer Chuck E. Chips, who would be late again, the 442nd time, for dinner and forget to call home; whose wife Mildred, at 9:15, would burn his portion of the meal, throw in the towel, and bid him adios; and whose limping badge was about to take off like a shooting star.

SLAMMER

Fatin Satin Aspen, reading *Fortune* magazine in the sanctuary of his bedroom, was not prepared for the five patrol cars, two canine units, and paddy wagon which converged at the front door of the school.

Sitting in the first patrol car, and leading the way, was a downtrodden, handcuffed Sweet Lou, who had been promised a reduced sentence of five to ten if he spilled the beans.

He not only spilled the beans, he opened the front door.

Bernadette Bagatelle, wandering down the hallway in search of a bedtime snack, ran into a manacled Sweet Lou, Officer Charles E. Chips of the highway patrol, and a pack of snarling German shepherds. Thinking "acid flashback," she continued steadfastly on her way.

Fatin Satin Aspen, hearing the thud of advancing boots and being no dummy, picked up the phone and called his attorney. With time off for good behavior, his attorney calculated, he could be out of the slammer in seven to ten years.

Officer Chuck E. Chips, flipping his nightstick through the air, read Fatin Satin Aspen his rights, mopped up the rest of the operation, and wondered what his wife Mildred had cooked for dinner.

HEADLINES

Ta Jan put on a kettle of water for coffee and walked sleepily to the front door. Killer Shep nuzzled warmly against her leg as she bent down and picked up the morning paper. Last night Ta Jan had dreamt that the number five and seven horses had come from behind to take the exacta at Golden Gate Fields. Zipping the rubber band into her neighbor's yard, she unfurled the paper and stared disbelievingly at the headline.

Walking rapidly back up the staircase, she opened doors, pulled down covers, and roused the rest of the household.

Dancer, Jessica, and the Kid staggered into the kitchen one by one and huddled grouchily over steaming cups of coffee.

"I have called you all together for this," Ta Jan gleefully exclaimed, slapping the front page of the newspaper in front of them.

The headline, in bold type of a size normally reserved for the words WAR or PEACE, read BOHEMIAN GROVE DE-FOLIATED.

STROKE OF LUCK

Over a breakfast of scrambled eggs, buckwheat pancakes, ham, and coffee, Ta Jan and Jessica listened attentively as Dancer and the Kid recounted what had taken place on their last foray into Fatin Satin Aspen's office.

"As we placed the roses with the note on his desk the Kid noticed the chart. We spread it out and realized that it must have been the topographical map of the Napa, Sonoma, and Mendocino counties."

"At a closer look, we noticed that some of the vineyards and their adjoining terrain lay between four adhesive-type dots," continued the Kid. "This was obviously the target area."

"But," Dancer said, "we needed help reading the coordinates, so—" she turned to Jessica—"we called Bucky."

"Bucky Benton?" Jessica exclaimed. "You called Bucky Benton from the office? What nerve!"

"I remembered Bucky had a pilot's license, so we called her and asked for help interpreting the coordinates."

"Then," said the Kid, "we removed the four red dots and repositioned them, as well as we could, at the location of the Bohemian Grove's 2500 acres. What we didn't know was that Fatin Satin Aspen's own vineyards bordered this region."

"A brilliant stroke of luck," cooed Ta Jan. "It says here in the paper that Luciano Davantini, the alleged pilot of the aircraft, sprayed the area continuously with the chemical Agent Orange until his tanks ran dry."

"Whew," exclaimed Dancer. "Remember those strange barrels in the wine cellar, Kid?"

The Kid quietly nodded.

"Listen to this," broke in Jessica. "It is believed that the accused Fatin Satin Aspen will be charged with unlawful labor practices, violation of customs regulations, and will be investigated for his alleged connections to a white slavery ring."

Killer Shep picked herself up from the kitchen floor and moved down the hallway. She had heard enough treachery and deceit to last for two lifetimes. Hopefully, for her, a second rebirth would not be necessary.

PARTINGS

The California Kid yawned lazily on the deck as the sun broke through the morning fog. She could hear Ta Jan and Jessica talking about old times in Hawaii. As she stretched her arms above her head, she felt a pair of hands encircle her wrists.

"Kid, why don't you come down to L.A. with us?" asked Dancer leaning against her shoulders. "Spend a couple of weeks, and enjoy the sun at Malibu."

"We'd love to have you," added a barefoot Jessica, stepping gingerly onto the redwood deck.

The Kid looked lustily at Jessica's emerald eyes and felt a twinge between her thighs. She reached into her pocket, unwrapped a wad of gum, and tossed it into her mouth. Chewing slowly, and choosing her words just as carefully, the Kid replied, "It's very kind of you both to offer, but Ta Jan has asked me to stay and give her a hand with the business. She said, Dancer, the minute we rolled into the Goose that first night, she was willing to propose we stay and learn the trade."

"No kidding," beamed Dancer, shading her eyes and placing an arm around Jessica's waist.

Jessica gazed past the warmth of the Kid's blue eyes. "Is it really the California Kid?" she shyly asked.

The California Kid put her feet up on the railing, leaned back into her chair, and stared thoughtfully at her two friends.

"It's Willy Gutherie," she said.

INVITATION

Three months later, on a cold and gloomy Saturday, the Kid received this postcard:

Dear Kid,
    Have just moved into the heart of LA. Lots of deli's, sun and local flavor. Please come and visit.

Jessica

The Kid tapped the card against her fingers. Lighting the last of her father's cigars, she opened a window and looked out over the gray city. Perhaps, she mused, it was time to see the "stuff" Hollywood was made of.

CLASSICS OF ASIAN AMERICAN LITERATURE

America Is in the Heart: A Personal History, by Carlos
  Bulosan, with a new introduction by Marilyn C.
  Alquizola and Lane Ryo Hirabayashi
Aiiieeeee! An Anthology of Asian American Writers, 3rd
  edition, edited by Frank Chin, Jeffery Paul Chan,
  Lawson Fusao Inada, and Shawn Hsu Wong, with a new
  foreword by Tara Fickle
Eat a Bowl of Tea, by Louis Chu, with a new foreword by
  Fae Myenne Ng and an introduction by Jeffery Paul
  Chan
Dancer Dawkins and the California Kid, by Willyce Kim,
  with a new preface by the author and a foreword by
  Eunsong Kim
Quiet Odyssey: A Pioneer Korean Woman in America, by
  Mary Paik Lee, edited with an introduction by Sucheng
  Chan, and a new foreword by David K. Yoo
Pangs of Love and Other Writings, by David Wong Louie,
  with a new foreword by Viet Thanh Nguyen and a new
  afterword by King-Kok Cheung

Photo by Campbell Crabtree

WILLYCE KIM is the author of three poetry books, *Curtains of Light, Eating Artichokes,* and *Under the Rolling Sky,* and two novels, *Dancer Dawkins and the California Kid* and *Dead Heat.* Her work has also appeared in journals including *The Furies, Phoenix Rising, Conditions, Sinister Wisdom, Harrington Lesbian Fiction Quarterly, Ikon,* and *Amazon Poetry.* Kim was an early member of the Women's Press Collective in Oakland, California, an organization that printed and distributed self-published books by lesbians. At the Women's Press Collective, Kim published her poetry, took photographs, and traveled the United States doing readings and distributing books in colleges, bookstores, and women's bars.